Can this romance be saved?

"You know what your problem is, Aaron?" Jessica demanded, her voice angry. "You are one of the most immature people I have ever met in my life."

"And you," Aaron said, "are one of the most stuck-up people I've ever met in mine."

Jessica heard a gasp from the next table. She glanced over and saw that Caroline Pearce was sitting there, her eyes wide, hanging on every word.

"Stuck-up?" she exclaimed, dropping her ice-cream cone on the table. She stood up, put her hands on her hips, and glared down at Aaron.

"Yeah," Aaron said, dropping his own cone and standing up to face her. "Look up the word 'snob' in the dictionary. You'll see your picture."

Jessica's whole body was shaking. How could Aaron be so mean? Why hadn't she realized this about him before?

"That's a big fat lie and you know it," she shouted. She was so angry now that she could hardly control herself. "I have news for you," she said slowly. "If this is the way you feel about me, then it's over. We're not going out anymore."

Aaron leaned across the table. His eyes locked onto hers. "Oh, yeah?" he answered evenly. "Who ever said we were?"

Bantam Books in the SWEET VALLEY TWINS AND FRIENDS series.
Ask your bookseller for the books you have missed.

#1	BEST FRIENDS	#41	THE TWINS GET CAUGHT
#2	TEACHER'S PET	#42	JESSICA'S SECRET
#3	THE HAUNTED HOUSE	#43	ELIZABETH'S FIRST KISS
#4	CHOOSING SIDES	#44	AMY MOVES IN
#5	SNEAKING OUT	#45	LUCY TAKES THE REINS
#6	THE NEW GIRL	#46	MADEMOISELLE JESSICA
#7	THREE'S A CROWD	#47	JESSICA'S NEW LOOK
#8	FIRST PLACE	#48	MANDY MILLER FIGHTS BACK
#9	AGAINST THE RULES	#49	THE TWINS' LITTLE SISTER
#10	ONE OF THE GANG	#50	JESSICA AND THE SECRET STAR
#11	BURIED TREASURE	#51	ELIZABETH THE IMPOSSIBLE
#12	KEEPING SECRETS	#52	BOOSTER BOYCOTT
#13	STRETCHING THE TRUTH	#53	THE SLIME THAT ATE SWEET VALLEY
#14	TUG OF WAR	#54	THE BIG PARTY WEEKEND
#15	THE OLDER BOY	#55	BROOKE AND HER ROCK-STAR MOM
#16	SECOND BEST	#56	THE WAKEFIELDS STRIKE IT RICH
#17	BOYS AGAINST GIRLS	#57	BIG BROTHER'S IN LOVE!
#18	CENTER OF ATTENTION	#58	ELIZABETH AND THE ORPHANS
#19	THE BULLY	#59	BARNYARD BATTLE
#20	PLAYING HOOKY	#60	CIAO, SWEET VALLEY!
#21	LEFT BEHIND	#61	JESSICA THE NERD
#22	OUT OF PLACE	#62	SARAH'S DAD AND SOPHIA'S MOM
#23	CLAIM TO FAME	#63	POOR LILA!
#24	JUMPING TO CONCLUSIONS	#64	THE CHARM SCHOOL MYSTERY
#25	STANDING OUT	#65	PATTY'S LAST DANCE
#26	TAKING CHARGE	#66	THE GREAT BOYFRIEND SWITCH
#27	TEAMWORK	#67	JESSICA THE THIEF
#28	APRIL FOOL!	#68	THE MIDDLE SCHOOL GETS MARRIED
#29	JESSICA AND THE BRAT ATTACK	#69	WON'T SOMEONE HELP ANNA?
#30	PRINCESS ELIZABETH	#70	PSYCHIC SISTERS
#31	JESSICA'S BAD IDEA	#71	JESSICA SAVES THE TREES
#32	JESSICA ON STAGE	#72	THE LOVE POTION
#33	ELIZABETH'S NEW HERO	#73	LILA'S MUSIC VIDEO
#34	JESSICA, THE ROCK STAR	#74	ELIZABETH THE HERO
#35	AMY'S PEN PAL	#75	JESSICA AND THE EARTHQUAKE
#36	MARY IS MISSING	#76	YOURS FOR A DAY
#37	THE WAR BETWEEN THE TWINS	#77	TODD RUNS AWAY
#38	LOIS STRIKES BACK	#78	STEVEN THE ZOMBIE
#39	JESSICA AND THE MONEY MIX-UP	#79	JESSICA'S BLIND DATE
#40	DANNY MEANS TROUBLE		

Sweet Valley Twins and Friends Super Editions

#1	THE CLASS TRIP	#3	THE BIG CAMP SECRET
#2	HOLIDAY MISCHIEF	#4	THE UNICORNS GO HAWAIIAN

Sweet Valley Twins and Friends Super Chiller Editions

#1	THE CHRISTMAS GHOST	#4	THE GHOST IN THE BELL TOWER
#2	THE GHOST IN THE GRAVEYARD	#5	THE CURSE OF THE RUBY NECKLACE
#3	THE CARNIVAL GHOST		

Sweet Valley Twins and Friends Magna Editions

THE MAGIC CHRISTMAS

A CHRISTMAS WITHOUT ELIZABETH

SWEET VALLEY TWINS
AND FRIENDS

Jessica's Blind Date

Written by
Jamie Suzanne

Created by
FRANCINE PASCAL

BANTAM BOOKS
NEW YORK•TORONTO•LONDON•SYDNEY•AUCKLAND

RL 4, 008-012

JESSICA'S BLIND DATE

A Bantam Book / May 1994

Sweet Valley High® and Sweet Valley Twins and Friends® are
registered trademarks of Francine Pascal

Conceived by Francine Pascal

Produced by Daniel Weiss Associates, Inc.
33 West 17th Street
New York, NY 10011

Cover art by James Mathewuse

ISBN: 0-553-48108-8

Published simultaneously in the United States and Canada

Bantam Books are published by Bantam Books, a division of Bantam
Doubleday Dell Publishing Group, Inc. Its trademark, consisting of the
words "Bantam Books" and the portrayal of a rooster, is Registered in
U.S. Patent and Trademark Office and in other countries. Marca
Registrada. Bantam Books, 1540 Broadway, New York, New York 10036.

PRINTED IN THE UNITED STATES OF AMERICA

OPM   0 9 8 7 6 5 4 3 2 1

To Briana Ferris Adler

One

◇

Jessica Wakefield sat picking at her taco. All around her in the Sweet Valley Middle School cafeteria, kids were laughing, joking, enjoying their lunches.

But not Jessica. She had spent most of the period so far staring into space with a frown on her face. Meanwhile, her best friends and her fellow members of the Unicorn Club were deeply involved in a discussion about Rick Hunter's upcoming party. Rick was the president of the seventh grade, and one of the cutest boys in the whole school. His party was big news, and normally Jessica would have been talking about it excitedly along with her friends. But today she had other things on her mind. She stabbed at her taco shell with her fork, distracted.

"What's the matter with you?" her friend Lila Fowler asked, finally noticing Jessica's silence.

"Nothing," Jessica muttered. That wasn't exactly true, but she wasn't sure she was ready to talk about what was bugging her, even with her best friends.

The problem was her sort-of boyfriend, Aaron Dallas. Recently Jessica had started noticing that a lot of the things he did got on her nerves. For instance, today he was wearing his dumb neon surfer shorts again. All the other guys in school had stopped wearing them months ago. Aaron didn't even seem to notice that they were totally out of style. Earlier that week when Jessica had subtly hinted that he might want to go shopping for some new clothes, he had just laughed and started teasing her about being a shopaholic. He obviously hadn't even thought about what she had said, since he was wearing the shorts again today. At times like this, Jessica found herself wondering why she had ever liked Aaron in the first place.

Jessica watched as Aaron pulled something from his lunch bag. *Oh, no. Graham crackers—again*, she thought unhappily. As if eating graham crackers weren't juvenile enough, he took one, crushed it in his hand, and poured the crumbs into his wide-open mouth. Jessica rolled her eyes and stifled a groan. Why did Aaron insist on acting like a six-year-old?

She noticed Aaron's friend Denny Jacobson unwrapping some homemade brownies. He immediately set one aside. Jessica knew he was saving it for his girlfriend, Janet Howell, the president of the Unicorns. *How romantic*, she thought. *Denny always thinks of Janet first. And* he *stopped wearing neon shorts months ago.*

Jessica sighed and picked up her taco, but she didn't have much of an appetite. Janet was so lucky. Not only was she one of the most beautiful and popular eighth graders in the school, but she also had one of the coolest boyfriends. Jessica glanced over at the boys' table again, comparing Denny's carefully combed short haircut with Aaron's rumpled, slightly too-long hair. She shook her head. How could she ever have thought Aaron's messy look was cute?

"So who are you going to Rick's party with, Jessica?" Ellen Riteman asked, breaking into Jessica's thoughts.

"I guess I'm going with Aaron," Jessica grumbled.

"You sound thrilled, Jess," Mandy Miller said jokingly.

"Really," Janet commented. She gave Jessica a curious look. "Aren't you and Aaron getting along these days?"

Jessica glanced across the lunchroom. "Look at his shorts."

Several of the Unicorns looked over.

"Hmmm. Good point," Ellen said. "It's weird. He used to be so cool."

"Don't be ridiculous, Ellen," Janet snapped. "Aaron is still cool, for a sixth grader at least. He's the star of the soccer team, he's cute—"

"His wardrobe stinks," Ellen finished helpfully.

"Come on, Ellen," Mandy chided. "It's not a crime to dress a little differently, you know." She smiled at Jessica, straightening the collar of her wildly patterned purple and black blouse. Mandy was known for her unusual outfits, which she put together from things she bought at thrift shops.

"That's right," Mary Wallace agreed, brushing back her long wavy blond hair. "As long as Jessica likes him, that's all that really matters."

Jessica sighed. "That's the problem. I'm not sure whether I like him so much anymore."

Janet turned and gazed at Aaron appraisingly. "Well," she said at last, "I still think Aaron is cool enough. But it couldn't hurt to look around and see what else is out there."

Ellen nodded wisely. "There are plenty of cute guys out there."

Jessica shrugged as she got up to leave. "Well, I'm not ready to do anything drastic," she said. "At least not before Rick's party."

When Aaron saw Jessica stand up he jumped up onto the bench he'd been sitting on and started waving wildly at her. "Yo, Jessica," he yelled. "Over here!"

Jessica gritted her teeth. " 'Bye, guys," she said to her friends. "Time to make my escape." She grabbed her lunch tray and headed for the garbage can farthest away from Aaron.

"Jessica!" he shouted again.

Out of the corner of her eye, Jessica could see Aaron waving his arms back and forth over his head. She hunched over, hoping he'd think she hadn't heard him, and kept moving.

She felt someone grab her arm. It was Caroline Pearce, the school gossip. "Jessica, Aaron's calling you."

"Thanks for telling me, Caroline," Jessica snapped impatiently. "I never would have known."

Caroline tightened her grip and raised her eyebrows curiously. "Is something going on between you two?"

Jessica forced herself to smile. Caroline wrote the gossip column for the *Sweet Valley Sixers*, the sixth-grade newspaper, and she liked nothing better than to start rumors. "No, nothing, Caroline," Jessica answered in her sweetest voice. "I just need to get out of here to, um, to go to the bathroom."

Jessica hurried into the hall before Caroline could answer. *Ah, safe at last.* She ducked her head and headed for the library. Aaron would never think to look for her in there.

Crash! Jessica was still staring at the floor when she ran headlong into her twin sister, Elizabeth, outside the library door.

"Ouch," Elizabeth said, rubbing her arm. "Watch where you're going, Jessica."

"Sorry," Jessica said.

"Since when are you in such a hurry to get to the library?" Elizabeth demanded. "Especially during lunch period?" She grinned. "I think this is a historic moment—I'm hurrying to get *out* of the library, and you're hurrying to get *in*."

Jessica grinned back in spite of herself. She had to admit that Elizabeth had a point. Even though Jessica and Elizabeth looked exactly alike—from their identical long blond hair and blue-green eyes to the dimple each twin had in her left cheek—anyone who knew them knew that was where the resemblance ended.

Jessica loved to spend her free time hanging out with the Unicorns, talking about boys, movies, and makeup. She hated to spend any time at all doing schoolwork—and the school library was just about the last place she'd be rushing to during lunch.

Elizabeth was just the opposite of her twin in many ways. She liked having fun, too, but she also enjoyed school and was proud of the good grades she earned. When she had some free time, she often spent it curled up alone with a good mystery novel or working on the *Sweet Valley Sixers*, the weekly newspaper she had helped start. But in spite of their differences, the twins were best friends.

"It's a long story," Jessica said. "I'll tell you later."

"Well, I'm glad I ran into you," Elizabeth said. "I have a question for you. Can you think of anyone who's good in science who could give Amy some extra help?" Amy Sutton was Elizabeth's best friend after Jessica. They worked together on the *Sixers*.

Jessica wasn't listening. She was too busy looking over her shoulder to see if Aaron was coming.

"Jessica? Did you hear me?"

"What?" She tried to remember Elizabeth's question. "A tutor, right?" She wrinkled her nose. "How should I know?"

She glanced down the hall again. *Uh-oh*. There was Aaron now, coming out of the cafeteria. He waved and started in her direction. "Um, I really have to go, Elizabeth," she said.

"Didn't Lila have someone helping her once?" Elizabeth asked. "I thought you mentioned a while ago that her father had hired a tutor for her."

Oh, no. He was getting closer. "Who?"

"Lila," Elizabeth repeated. She was starting to sound annoyed. She took a step closer. "Jessica! What's with you? I was hoping you could ask Lila how she found her tutor. Or maybe you could see if any of the other Unicorns have any suggestions."

Jessica lost her patience. "Elizabeth! If Amy needs a tutor, why don't you just put up a sign or advertise in your newspaper? I really have to go, OK?"

But it was too late. Aaron had caught up to her. "Hiya, Jess Wess."

Jessica cringed. *Jess Wess?* she thought irritably. *Where did he come up with that?* "Hi, Aaron," she replied glumly.

"Hi, Aaron," Elizabeth said more politely.

Aaron grinned at them both, then turned to Jessica. "Where'd you go? I wanted to ask you something."

"About what?" Jessica said. She took several steps backward. She didn't want to be seen standing too close to him while he was wearing those ridiculous shorts.

"I wanted to see if you felt like going to Casey's for ice cream after school," Aaron said. Casey's was an ice-cream parlor at the Valley Mall where a lot of the middle schoolers liked to hang out.

"Ummm." Jessica thought fast. Maybe there was some way she could get him to change clothes before they went.

Aaron gave her his lopsided grin. "Pretty please? We can share a Casey's Special."

"*Pretty please?*" *Ugh.* "That sounds like a lot of ice cream," Jessica said out loud, hoping Aaron would change his mind about wanting to go.

"Then you can order something else," Aaron said with a shrug.

Jessica sighed. Obviously Aaron wasn't capable of taking a hint. "Oh, OK," she said. "I'll meet you there at four."

"Great," Aaron said cheerfully. He waved goodbye to both twins and ambled off.

"What's going on?" Elizabeth demanded as soon as he was out of earshot.

"What do you mean?" Jessica said innocently.

"Why were you so mean to Aaron?"

"Oh, that," Jessica said evasively.

"I think you hurt his feelings," Elizabeth said.

Jessica ignored Elizabeth's comment. "Did you see those shorts he was wearing? No one wears neon shorts anymore. Aaron used to be so cool. I don't understand what happened to him."

Elizabeth rolled her eyes. "Jessica! A person's shorts is no reason to stop liking them."

"But there's more, Lizzie," Jessica cried defensively. "Believe me, it goes *way* beyond the shorts." She started in on a list of Aaron's many faults, from his immature behavior to his weird hairdo to the powdered graham crackers.

"But you're forgetting something, Jess," Elizabeth said when her twin had finished.

Jessica folded her arms. It was really annoying sometimes the way Elizabeth always insisted on giving everyone the benefit of the doubt. "What?"

"Remember last week? Aaron gave you his old soccer jersey *and* the latest Johnny Buck CD."

"True," said Jessica slowly. She'd slept in the jersey every single night for the past week. It even had Aaron's team number on it. The Johnny Buck CD was pretty cool, too. It was his latest album, *Getting Tough*, and Jessica had listened to nothing else for a week.

"I guess you have a point, Lizzie," Jessica admitted thoughtfully. "Aaron can be a lot of fun when he's not being a dork. And he's obviously crazy about me. Tomorrow he'll be wearing a different pair of shorts, and we can always hope he'll remember to comb his hair."

"That's the attitude, Jess," Elizabeth said. "You shouldn't just write him off. You guys are the perfect couple. Everybody says so."

"I know," Jessica said modestly.

Elizabeth was right. Jessica *was* overreacting. She shouldn't dump Aaron because of some stupid shorts. Besides, she didn't want to have to worry about finding another date for Rick's party.

Two

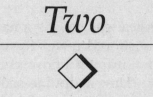

Casey's was packed when Jessica arrived. She waved to Mandy and Ellen, who were sitting together at a table near the door. At another table she saw Janet sitting with Denny. Jessica scanned the rest of the room. Where was Aaron?

She finally spotted him standing by the counter. She smiled. He was wearing a different pair of shorts.

She came up behind him. "Hi," she said, tugging on his T-shirt.

Aaron spun around. "Hi, yourself," he answered.

Jessica nearly fainted. Aaron was wearing a Donald Duck T-shirt!

"Like my new shirt?" he said. "I think it's hilarious."

Hilarious if you're four years old, Jessica thought irritably. Her first instinct had been right. She should have tried harder to think of an excuse not to come.

"What kind of ice cream do you want?" Aaron asked.

"Um . . ." Jessica was having a hard time concentrating now. She should never have listened to her twin. What did Elizabeth know about this kind of thing, anyway? "Um, a double-scoop fudge swirl cone," she said to the woman behind the counter.

"Great," Aaron said. "I'll have a double scoop of bubble gum with rainbow sprinkles on top."

Bubble gum with sprinkles? Was he for real? Jessica grabbed the cone the woman was holding out and headed for the only empty table left, which was near the center of the room. After Aaron had paid for the cones, he joined her there. As soon as he sat down he started humming the theme from *The Flinstones*.

"Do you have to hum that?" Jessica said.

"What do you want me to hum?" Aaron asked.

"Something that isn't in reruns," Jessica snapped.

Aaron shrugged and stopped humming. Instead, he concentrated on his ice cream. He licked around the edges of the cone, trying to stop the ice cream that was melting and running down onto his hand. *Slurp, slurp.*

Jessica pretended not to notice him.

"Oh, Jess Wess," he said. Now he was taking big

goofy slurps from his cone. He obviously thought it made him look cute and adorable.

"Stop that," Jessica said with a frown. She was becoming more annoyed by the second.

"What?" Aaron said. *Slurp.*

"You're slurping," Jessica said.

Aaron grinned. "So?" *Slurp, slurp.*

"So it's disgusting."

Aaron didn't say anything. Instead, he licked a bunch of sprinkles off the top of the cone. Then he stuck out his sprinkle-covered tongue at Jessica.

"Stop it!" Jessica shouted. What was with Aaron lately? He never used to be this way. Now every single thing he did or said seemed designed to irritate her as much as possible.

Aaron swallowed the sprinkles. "What's your problem today, anyway?"

Jessica couldn't believe it. "*My* problem?"

"Yeah. You've been grouchy all day."

Jessica pursed her lips. "You'd be grouchy, too, if the person you went out with wore neon shorts and stupid Donald Duck T-shirts."

Aaron looked down at his shirt. "I happen to like this T-shirt." His eyes narrowed. "At least everything I own isn't *purple*."

Now he was criticizing *her* clothes? Jessica had always prided herself on her excellent taste. "Purple is the official color of the Unicorns," she said through gritted teeth. "You know that."

"Yeah, well, I hate to tell you, but it's not really your color," Aaron said with a shrug.

Jessica could feel her blood pressure rising. How dare he criticize her? And since when didn't he like the way she dressed? She'd always thought that Aaron considered her to be perfect. Now she was learning the cold truth. Well, if that was the way he felt, she was going to tell him exactly how she felt about *him*.

"You know what your problem is, Aaron?" she demanded, her voice angry. "You are one of the most immature people I have ever met in my life."

"And you," Aaron said, "are one of the most stuck-up people I've ever met in mine."

Jessica heard a gasp from the next table. She glanced over and saw that Caroline Pearce was sitting there, her eyes wide, hanging on every word. Jessica was so angry she didn't care if the whole world was listening.

"Stuck-up?" she exclaimed, dropping her ice-cream cone on the table. She stood up, put her hands on her hips, and glared down at Aaron.

"Yeah," Aaron said, dropping his own cone and standing up to face her. "Look up the word 'snob' in the dictionary. You'll see your picture."

Jessica felt her face grow hot. "At least I don't stand on chairs in the lunchroom and hoot at people to get their attention."

A few people in the room laughed. Jessica realized that the whole restaurant was listening to their fight.

Aaron sneered. "You're lucky I'm even *paying* attention to you, Jessica. After all, if I didn't, nobody else would."

Jessica's whole body was shaking. How could Aaron be so mean? Why hadn't she realized this about him before?

"That's a big fat lie and you know it," she shouted. She was so angry now that she could hardly control herself. "I have news for you," she said slowly. "If this is the way you feel about me, then it's over. We're not going out anymore."

Aaron leaned across the table. His eyes locked onto hers. "Oh, yeah?" he answered evenly. "Who ever said we were?"

Jessica clenched her fists. Without another word, she stormed out the door.

Elizabeth was sitting at the kitchen table working on the next edition of the *Sixers* when Jessica burst into the room. "Hi, Jess," she said, looking up. "What's the matter?"

Jessica threw herself into the chair beside Elizabeth's. "It's over," she exclaimed. "Finished."

Elizabeth was used to Jessica's theatrics. "What's over?" she asked patiently.

"Oh, Lizzie, it was awful," Jessica said, her eyes welling up with tears. "Aaron and I had a big fight. He called me a snob. Can you believe it?"

Elizabeth didn't answer. Jessica and Aaron had fights all the time. Jessica always overreacted,

Aaron always apologized, and then everything was fine again. Elizabeth had learned that it was usually better not to offer any advice or comment on anything her sister said about Aaron. She gently moved Jessica's elbow aside. "Excuse me, you're leaning on the scissors."

"Not only that. He humiliated me in front of everyone at Casey's," Jessica continued. "If I never see Aaron Dallas again in my life, it will be too soon. It's really over this time."

"You mean you broke up?" Elizabeth asked.

"For good," Jessica said.

"I'm sorry, Jess," Elizabeth replied, giving her twin a sympathetic look. "But I'll bet you guys can work things out." She reached across the table for the tape.

"Aren't you listening to me? I don't *want* to work things out," Jessica said. "It was a giant mistake ever to go out with Aaron in the first place." She crossed her arms and stared at Elizabeth. "What are you working on, anyway?" She sounded exasperated. "You seem awfully busy."

"I am," Elizabeth said. "You gave me a great idea earlier. Remember when I asked if you knew anyone who could give Amy some extra help in science? You said she should try advertising, and that's what she's going to do. The *Sixers* is starting its own classified advertising section."

"Oh," Jessica said, trying to sound interested. "That's nice, I guess."

"It'll be great," Elizabeth said. "I'm going to place an ad to try to sell my old typewriter, since I do all my writing on the computer now." She held up an old shoe box. "See this? Each advertiser will have a box in the *Sixers* office for any responses. That way ads can be anonymous if people want. People will be able to sell or find whatever they need through the *Sixers*."

"Sounds good, Lizzie," Jessica said, shoving back her chair. She stood up. "Unfortunately, that doesn't help me with my problem."

"Sorry, Jess," Elizabeth said, looking up from her work. "I know you don't feel like talking about the paper when you're so upset about breaking up with Aaron."

"You're not kidding," Jessica said, stomping away toward the stairs. "Now I have to find a new date for Rick's party."

That night Jessica lay in bed tossing and turning. Every time she thought about her fight with Aaron she felt angry all over again. She couldn't believe she'd been so blind to Aaron's faults. How could she ever have liked him?

At least it was finished now. Over. She was free.

She sighed and kicked off the covers. Now she had a new problem, though. She wasn't about to show up alone at Rick's party. She had to find a date.

Maybe she should skip the party. She could pretend to come down with the flu. That excuse hardly ever worked when she was trying to get out of school, but she doubted her parents would be suspicious if she was missing a party.

Jessica sat up and pounded her fist in the covers. No! It wasn't fair. She had really been looking forward to Rick's party. And now Aaron had ruined it for her. She would never forgive him for this. She threw herself back onto the pillows. There had to be *something* she could do. . . .

Jessica sat up again. Suddenly she remembered something Elizabeth had said that afternoon. Slowly Jessica's expression changed from angry to thoughtful to triumphant. Hadn't Elizabeth said that with the classified ads people would be able to find anything they needed through the *Sixers*?

I know exactly *what I need!* Jessica thought with a sly grin.

Three

◇

"Good morning," Jessica said cheerfully as she bounded into the kitchen the next morning. She came up behind her mother, who was scrambling eggs at the stove, and planted a big kiss on her cheek. "Mmmm, those eggs smell delicious."

"Thanks, sweetie," Mrs. Wakefield said. She gave Jessica a curious expression. "You sure are in a good mood today, aren't you?"

"Yep. A great mood." She leaned over her father, who was reading the paper. "Can I pour you some more coffee, Dad?"

Mr. Wakefield shot Mrs. Wakefield a puzzled look. "Sure. Thanks."

Jessica's older brother, Steven, looked up from his orange juice. "OK, Jess. What do you want from them? Money? More purple jeans?"

Jessica gave him her sunniest smile. "Very funny, Steven. I'm allowed to be in a good mood if I want," she said, pouring herself a glass of milk."

"Oh, yeah?" Steven said, raising one eyebrow. "I would think you'd be depressed about your big fight scene at Casey's yesterday."

Jessica's smile faded a little bit. "How did you hear about that?"

"Oh, come on, Jessica! The whole town has heard about it by now," Steven replied with a laugh.

"Shut up, Steven," Jessica grumbled. "Where's Elizabeth?" she asked, trying to change the subject before her parents asked any questions.

"She hasn't come down yet," Mr. Wakefield replied.

"Did I hear my name?" Elizabeth asked as she walked into the kitchen.

"Oh, Lizzie, there you are!" Jessica exclaimed, her cheerful mood back instantly.

"Good morning, Jess," Elizabeth replied, giving her twin a quizzical look as she walked to the refrigerator. "You're in a good mood today."

"That's because I've figured out the answer to all my problems," Jessica told her.

Steven hooted. "This should be good."

Jessica glared at him, then turned to her twin. "I'll tell you on the way to school, Elizabeth," she said pointedly. "When there are no morons around to interrupt us."

When Elizabeth had finally finished her breakfast, Jessica practically dragged her out of the house. "It's about time," she exclaimed when they were outside on the sidewalk. "I thought you were going to eat everything in the whole house!"

"Since when are you in such a big hurry to get to school?" Elizabeth demanded.

"I just couldn't wait to tell you my brilliant plan," Jessica said.

"What brilliant plan?" Elizabeth asked suspiciously. Jessica's plans often landed the two of them in trouble.

"I'll show you," Jessica said. She reached into her pocket for the slip of paper she'd been carrying around all morning. With a flourish, she handed it to Elizabeth.

"What's this?" Elizabeth asked.

"Read it," Jessica urged her. "It's for the new *Sixers* classified section."

"'Gorgeous, sophisticated blonde seeks boyfriend,'" Elizabeth read aloud. "'Loves rock music, Doc Martens, beach parties, and airplane food. Hates square dancing, itchy sweaters, and black jellybeans. Please respond to box number one.'"

Jessica smiled proudly. She had spent almost an hour on the wording of the ad the night before.

Elizabeth frowned. "Jess, no way. This isn't a classified ad. This is a personal ad."

"That's OK," Jessica said with a shrug. "You can put it with the classifieds."

Elizabeth shook her head. "No," she said firmly. "I can't put this in the paper."

Jessica's face fell. "Why not?"

"Because it's . . . a joke, that's why."

Jessica felt insulted. "There's nothing funny about not having a date for Rick's party, Elizabeth," she snapped. "Anyway, what's the difference between advertising for a tutor and advertising for a boyfriend?"

"There's a big difference," Elizabeth said. "A newspaper is supposed to print important stuff."

"This *is* important," Jessica insisted. "It's way more important than those stupid lunch menus, and you always print those."

Elizabeth threw up her arms. "Great. The next thing you know, all the Unicorns are going to be advertising for dates."

"No, they won't," Jessica said. "No one will know it's me. The ad is anonymous."

"That's not the point," Elizabeth said. "Something like this changes the whole tone of the newspaper. It goes from being serious to being silly."

"No, it doesn't," Jessica said. "We're only talking about a couple of lines, not the whole paper. What's the big deal?"

Elizabeth reread the ad and sighed. "I really think this is a bad idea," she said.

Jessica paused. She didn't want to start a fight with Elizabeth right now, or she'd never agree to print the ad. "Pleeeeeeease, Lizzie?" she said sweetly. "Just a couple little lines. Hardly anyone will even notice."

Elizabeth sighed again. "OK, Jess. I'll print the ad. You're right. A couple lines can't be that big a deal."

When Jessica sat down for lunch that day at the Unicorner, the table where the Unicorns always sat, the first thing everyone wanted to hear about was about her big fight with Aaron.

"Jessica, I couldn't believe my ears at Casey's yesterday," Janet said. "You really let Aaron have it."

"I can't believe you guys broke up," Mandy said. "Is it really over?"

"For good," Jessica said. "Period. The end." She gave a dramatic sigh, pleased to be the center of attention.

Mary shook her head in disbelief. "I really thought you guys would be together for a long time," she said. "You seemed to be so perfect for each other."

"Yeah, well, things change," Jessica said philosophically. "I used to think his clowning around was cute. But now I realize it's just been covering up what an immature jerk he was all along."

"But who are you going to take to Rick Hunter's party?" Lila asked.

Jessica shrugged. She enjoyed having her friends' sympathy, but she didn't want them to think she was desperate or anything. "Someone better will turn up."

"Who?" Grace Oliver asked.

"There are plenty of guys out there. I just have to decide which one I want." Jessica smiled to herself. Now that she was running a personals ad, she wasn't worried at all.

"Well, keep your eyes off Jake," Lila said. "Our one-month anniversary is coming up in two days."

A hush fell over the table.

"Really?" Ellen breathed. "That's so romantic! What are you going to do to celebrate?"

Lila stared dreamily into space. "I'm sure Jake has all kinds of romantic things planned." She fluttered her eyelids. "He's so wonderful. . . . He's kind, considerate . . ."

"Cute," Janet said.

They all giggled.

"Maybe he'll bring you flowers," Tamara Chase said.

"Flowers are nice," Janet said. "But he'd better do something a little more special than that for your anniversary." She smiled. "I remember on my one-month anniversary with Denny we went for a moonlight walk on the beach. He brought a picnic. It was so romantic."

"Isn't that when you got food poisoning from the mayonnaise?" Ellen said.

Janet frowned. "Why do you always bring that up, Ellen?" she snapped. "Anyway, he also gave me my locket that night." She fingered the tiny silver locket around her neck.

"Wow," Mandy said. "Denny really is incredible. Peter hasn't given me anything." She stared at her boyfriend Peter Jeffries, who was sitting across the room.

"Neither has Winston," Grace said, glancing over at Winston Egbert, who was sitting with Peter, Denny, and Aaron. "Except a book about the constellations. And once he took me to the zoo."

They all laughed.

"Remember, you guys haven't been going out for all that long," Lila said. "When you've been together as long as Jake and I have, maybe you'll have better luck." She sighed. "Then again, there aren't many guys like Jake."

A loud commotion erupted on the other side of the cafeteria. "What's going on?" Mandy asked. All the Unicorns turned to look.

"It's a food fight," Lila announced.

They all watched as Peter Jeffries chucked a slice of bread at Denny Jacobson. The bread bounced off Denny's head and fell into Aaron's lap. Aaron shot a spoonful of applesauce back at Denny, who crumbled up his remaining potato chips and drizzled them into Winston Egbert's hair.

"Gross," Jessica said.

"Completely," Janet agreed.

Mandy shook her head. "Kind of makes you wonder what we see in them, doesn't it?"

That afternoon Elizabeth was sitting in the *Sixers*

office staring at the computer screen when Amy walked in.

"Hi, Elizabeth," Amy said. "Are you ready to start running off copies of this week's edition?"

"Oh, hi," Elizabeth said, looking up. "I'm glad you're here. I was just trying to set up the new classified section on the screen and I need your advice."

"Hmmm," Amy said, studying the layout on the computer screen. "Looks OK. Kind of boring, though."

The word CLASSIFIED was neatly centered at the top of the page. Amy and Elizabeth's two ads were listed below the headline.

"I agree," Elizabeth said with a thoughtful frown. "It needs to be jazzed up." She fiddled with the border. "Part of the problem is this computer program. It can only do so much." She sighed and erased the border.

"What's this?" Amy asked, picking up a piece of paper lying beside the computer.

Elizabeth tried putting the heading in italics. "What?" she asked, her eyes still focused on the screen.

"'Gorgeous, sophisticated blonde seeks boyfriend.'" Amy looked up from Jessica's ad. "This is some kind of joke, right?"

"I wish," Elizabeth said ruefully.

Amy's eyes grew wide. "You're not serious, are you? I thought you and Todd were really happy together."

"What?" Elizabeth said. "Ohhh." Her face turned red. "It's not for me. It's Jessica's. She wants to put it in the classified section."

"Jessica wrote a personals ad?" Amy exclaimed. "How embarrassing."

Elizabeth shrugged. "I don't know why I agreed to print it."

Amy read the ad again. "Does this have anything to do with the scene at Casey's yesterday?" Amy asked.

"Yeah. She wants to find a new boyfriend to take to Rick Hunter's party. But it's supposed to be anonymous, so don't tell anyone it's her, OK?"

"All right," Amy said doubtfully. "But it's not exactly hard to guess who it is."

"Oh, I don't know," Elizabeth said with a smile. "After all, you thought it was me." Then her smile faded. "But seriously, Amy, what do you think about the paper running a personals ad?"

"Honestly?"

Elizabeth nodded. She trusted Amy's opinion a lot, especially when it came to things like this.

"I think it's unprofessional," Amy said. "This is supposed to be a serious newspaper. *The New York Times* doesn't carry personals. Something like this makes the whole paper seem less serious somehow. You know, less reliable or something."

"That's what I think, too," Elizabeth said grimly. "I knew I shouldn't have said yes to Jessica." She shook her head. "Oh, well. I'm sure Jessica will realize it was a mistake when she sees it in print."

Amy shrugged and didn't answer. Instead, she leaned over Elizabeth's shoulder to look again at the classified section on the computer screen. "Where were you planning to put Jessica's ad?"

"Maybe at the bottom of the page," Elizabeth said. "I promised I'd print it, but not that I'd give it a front-page headline." She quickly typed it in.

She and Amy spent a few more minutes experimenting with the layout of the page. When they were satisfied that it looked as good as it was going to look, they printed out the whole issue and read it through one last time.

"Perfect," Amy announced as she finished proofreading the last page. "Let's run it off and get out of here."

They headed for the photocopy machine in the school office. By the next morning, copies of that week's edition, including Jessica's ad, would be available for the taking. Elizabeth crossed her fingers and hoped she hadn't made a mistake.

Four

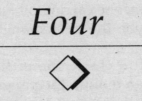

Elizabeth's friend Maria Slater stopped her in the hallway the next day after third period. "Hey, Elizabeth, why didn't you put out a paper this week?" Maria asked.

"What do you mean?" Elizabeth said. "Copies are stacked inside every homeroom, as usual."

"I didn't see any in Mrs. Thompson's class," Maria said.

"That's strange. I know there were some there this morning," Elizabeth said. "Maybe they're all gone."

She stuck her head into a nearby classroom. No papers.

"I don't understand," Elizabeth said. "We printed the same number we always do, and we've never run out before."

"Oh, well," Maria said. "If you track one down, save it for me, OK?" She waved good-bye and headed for her next class.

But Elizabeth stood still in the middle of the hallway, trying to figure out what could have happened. Had someone carried off all the newspapers as a joke? Maybe the custodian had tossed them out by mistake.

She decided to check one of the seventh-grade classrooms. Even though the paper was distributed schoolwide, most of its readers were sixth graders, and there were always plenty of leftovers in the seventh- and eighth-grade homerooms.

As Elizabeth reached the nearest seventh-grade classroom, she noticed a group of students clustered outside, talking and laughing noisily. "Excuse me," she said, squeezing past. She noticed that two or three people were holding copies of the *Sixers*.

Then Elizabeth heard Jake Hamilton say to one of the other boys, "Gorgeous Blonde will never go for you, Smith. You eat so many black jellybeans, I'm surprised your teeth haven't turned black." The rest of the group hooted with laughter.

Elizabeth froze.

"Not true," the second boy said, still laughing. "I never eat jellybeans and you know it. But I do eat airplane food."

Elizabeth couldn't believe her ears. Was she hallucinating, or were they all talking about Jessica's ad? She stuck her head inside the classroom door and checked for extra papers. There were only two copies left. She picked one up for Maria and then stood still for another moment, listening.

"Bruce likes airplane food, too, don't you, Bruce?" Rick Hunter was saying.

"True," Bruce Patman replied. "And I like gorgeous blondes even better."

"Who do you think it is?" Tamara Chase asked excitedly. "Keri Thompkins is blond."

"So is half the school," Rick replied.

"It's nobody," another girl said. "Don't you get it? It's a big joke."

"Some joke," one of the boys said. "Maybe it's Madonna."

They all howled with laughter.

The bell rang. Elizabeth tried to collect her thoughts. Were all the newspapers gone because people had taken them to read Jessica's ad? Could people really be that interested in a silly personal ad?

Just then the bell rang, and Elizabeth realized she would have to hurry if she didn't want to be late for her next class. Ducking her head, she pushed her way through the crowded hallway. "Excuse me, please," she mumbled. "Excuse me." She looked up. A boy whose name she didn't know caught her eye. He had brown eyes and dark curly hair. "Sorry," she said, trying to get past him.

He looked at her strangely, then grinned. "That's OK, gorgeous." He was holding the newspaper in his hand.

Suddenly Elizabeth had a terrible thought. *He must be wondering if I'm the one who placed that ad! How embarrassing!*

Elizabeth focused her eyes on the floor and rushed past him. She could hear people all around her talking about Jessica's ad.

She stalked into her fourth-period study hall and threw down her books. She knew she shouldn't have let Jessica talk her into putting that ridiculous ad in the paper. She had been right all along. It was turning the *Sweet Valley Sixers* into a giant joke.

Jessica flipped impatiently through her social studies book that afternoon. She tried to appear interested in what Mrs. Arnette was saying, but in reality she had other things on her mind. She'd barely been in school five minutes today when she'd heard people talking about her personal ad. It seemed as if everyone was talking about it. At lunch it had been the main topic of conversation at the Unicorner. Everyone had a different theory about who had written the ad. Jessica had pretended not to know any more than anyone else—even when Janet had said that Gorgeous Blonde was probably an eighth grader, since the ad sounded mature. It was so tempting to tell them it was her!

Jessica stared at the clock and swung her legs back and forth under her chair. Only five minutes to go until the final bell. She couldn't wait for school to end so she could check the response box she had placed in the *Sixers* office. She figured that dozens of cute boys had probably already written to her, since the ad was the talk of the school.

When the bell finally rang, she flew out of the room, practically colliding with Mandy. "Oh, sorry. Are you OK?" she exclaimed.

"Not really," Mandy replied. "But it's not your fault."

Jessica noticed that her friend's usually cheerful face was gloomy. In fact, Mandy looked as though she was about to cry. "What's the matter?" Jessica asked.

Mandy glanced around the hall, then lowered her voice. "Come into the bathroom and I'll tell you. I don't want Peter to hear me."

Jessica may have been in a big hurry, but this sounded like something serious. She followed Mandy into the girls' bathroom. "What happened?"

Mandy took a deep breath. "Peter told me he likes somebody else."

"You're kidding!" Jessica said. "Who?"

"He won't tell me." She glanced around nervously. "All he'll say is that it's someone who he thinks has more in common with him than I do." She sniffled forlornly.

"Maybe whoever it is won't like him back," Jessica said hopefully, handing Mandy a tissue.

"Maybe," Mandy said. She accepted the tissue and blew her nose. Then she thought for a moment.

"Or maybe it wouldn't be such a bad thing if we did break up. All we ever do together is go to kung fu movies. I hate kung fu movies. Everyone always gets killed."

Jessica tried to remember what movie she and Aaron had seen the last time they had gone to the movies with Mandy and Peter. Then she remembered. *Chinese War Dragons*.

"I'm sorry, Mandy," Jessica said sympathetically. "Somehow I thought you and Peter would be a couple forever." *Just like me and Aaron*, she added to herself.

"Me, too," Mandy said with a sniff.

Jessica talked to Mandy for a few more minutes, trying to cheer her up. When Mandy left to head home, Jessica hurried on to her locker, got her things together, and then rushed to the *Sixers* office.

She burst inside, then stopped short. "Oh, hi."

Elizabeth's friend Sophia Rizzo was working at the computer. She looked up and smiled at Jessica. "Hi. Are you looking for Elizabeth?"

"Not really," Jessica said, trying to sound casual. She hadn't thought about running into people. How was she supposed to check her responses with Sophia sitting there watching her? She didn't want Sophia telling everyone that Jessica was the one who had placed the ad.

Jessica sneaked a glance at her response box. She could see something inside. She gritted her teeth, then forced herself to smile as she turned back to

Sophia. "Elizabeth *is* looking for *you*, though."

Sophia looked surprised. "She is? But she was just here."

Jessica thought fast. "I know. But she said she forgot to tell you something important. Something *really* important. She didn't tell me what it was about, though."

Sophia seemed to be thinking this information over. "Maybe it has to do with this article I'm finishing on boys' basketball."

"You never know," Jessica said. "But there's still time to catch her. She's in the—" Jessica picked the farthest spot she could think of. "In the gym."

Sophia pushed her chair back. "Maybe I should go see what she wants."

Jessica breathed a sigh of relief. "Good idea." She stood in the hall until she was sure Sophia was gone, then hurried back inside.

Shaking with excitement, Jessica reached into her response box. She pulled out a fistful of folded papers, all addressed to "Box #1." She counted them aloud. "One, two, three, four, five, six." *Not a bad start*, she thought. She quickly stuffed all six responses into her backpack. She would take them home and read them in privacy.

As Jessica left the office she saw Lila coming down the hallway in her direction, looking incredibly happy. "Hi, Lila. Where are you going?" she asked curiously.

Lila danced from one foot to the other. "Home to

change clothes," she said. "I'm supposed to meet Jake at Casey's in one hour. This is our one-month anniversary, remember?"

"Oh, right," Jessica said. "Have fun."

"Do you think I should wear my black miniskirt and a red sweater or my purple leggings with the white tunic?" Lila asked.

Lila had millions of outfits, and at the moment Jessica couldn't remember any of them. All she could think about was getting home to read her responses. "Whatever," she answered.

"Or maybe my new lavender dress," Lila said. "Do you think Jake would think it was too dressy?"

"How should I know?" Jessica said.

Lila tossed her head. "Fine," she snapped. "I know you're distracted over this boyfriend thing and all, but you could at least pretend to be interested in my anniversary. I mean it's only one of the most important days of my life, you know."

"Sorry, Lila, you're right," Jessica said. "I think you should go with the black miniskirt. It looks really good on you."

"Oh, all right," Lila said, seeming satisfied with the apology. "Thanks for the advice."

"Hey, what are friends for?" Jessica replied. "Have fun with Jake!" She hurried off, breathing a sigh of relief.

As soon as Jessica got home she headed straight for her room. She locked the door, then carefully spread her responses out on her bed. She picked up the one closest to her.

"Dear Gorgeous Blonde—If you're serious, so am I." Jessica smiled. Pretty good start. She read on: he was in seventh grade, had dark hair, liked to watch scary movies and . . . oh, yuck. He played hockey. She hated hockey.

Jessica went on to the second guy. She unfolded his response and frowned. He'd written his letter on a piece of paper torn out of a notebook. It looked really messy. And if his letter was this messy, he probably was, too. She looked around her room at piles of dirty clothes and an overflowing wastebasket. One messy person was enough in any relationship. She tossed the second letter on top of the first and moved on to the next one.

Number three was neatly typed and started off with a poem: "Roses are red, violets are blue, Gorgeous, I'd be honored to meet with you." She glanced at the bottom of the page. Oh, no! Number three actually gave his identity—it was Donald Zwerdling. Jessica winced. Was he kidding? The geek with bright red hair and glasses? She dropped his letter like a hot potato.

The fourth guy started off by describing himself as a computer nut. Then he started telling her about all his favorite video games and what level he'd reached on each of them. "I don't think so," Jessica muttered, tossing it onto the reject pile.

Number five sounded nice but a little boring. He

wrote that he liked to read, watch TV, and play with his dog. Jessica hated dogs. She tossed that note aside, too. *After all, I'm allowed to be choosy,* she thought.

Number six was really a joke. The handwriting was so messy that Jessica could hardly decipher the opening lines. "Dear Blind Babe," it said. She squinted at the scrawled words. No, wait. "*Blond* Babe." She waded through the next two lines. "You sound like lots of fin." Fun? "I like to potty, too." Party maybe? She giggled and put the paper down. Forget that one.

Jessica stared at her first day's collection, a little disappointed. Oh, well, she told herself. The really cool boys probably didn't want to sound too anxious by responding on the first day. Maybe she'd have better luck tomorrow.

Five

◇

The next morning Jessica cruised into school twenty minutes early. She headed straight for the *Sixers* office, but there was nothing new in the response box yet. For a second Jessica was worried, but when she thought about it she realized there hadn't really been time for anyone to respond since the afternoon before. By the end of the day she was sure to have more notes.

She killed some time in the bathroom fixing her hair, then wandered to her locker. The hallways were beginning to fill up. Soon the first-period bell rang. Jessica got her books together and started down the hall. A figure dressed in black and wearing dark glasses approached her. "Hello, Jessica."

Jessica peered at the mysterious figure, then gasped. "Lila! Is that you? What's wrong?"

Lila removed her dark glasses. Her eyes were red and puffy, obviously from crying. "He forgot," she announced in a hollow voice.

"Who forgot? What?" Jessica said.

Lila's shoulders slumped. "Jake," she said, choking back a sob. "He forgot our one-month anniversary."

Jessica gave her friend a hug. "Oh, Lila. That's awful!"

Lila nodded and reached into her purse for a tissue. "I looked fantastic, too. I wore the black miniskirt like you suggested."

"So did he just never show up, or what?"

Lila shook her head. "When I got to Casey's he was there all right, but he was sitting with half the basketball team. They were trying to see who could shoot a paper straw the farthest." She sniffled. "I sat there waiting, thinking something was going to happen, like maybe he had some big romantic surprise planned and was just trying to catch me off guard, you know? But finally he just stood up and announced that it was time for him to go home for dinner."

"What a jerk," Jessica said. "Did you say anything to him?"

"Of course I did. I said, 'What about our anniversary?' and he said, 'What anniversary?'" A tear rolled slowly down Lila's cheek.

Jessica could tell that Lila needed her help, and luckily she knew just what to do. "Listen, Lila," she said. "You don't need Jake. You should find your-self a new boyfriend."

"A new boyfriend?" Lila sniffled again.

Jessica nodded. If it worked for her, why couldn't it work for Lila, too? There were plenty of guys to go around. "You know that new classified section in the *Sixers*?" she said in a low voice. "You can advertise there for a new boyfriend."

"Oh, please, Jessica," Lila said, rolling her eyes. "I'm not that desperate. I don't have to *advertise* to get dates like that loser who calls herself Gorgeous Blonde." She laughed. "If she's that gorgeous, she'd already have a boyfriend!"

Jessica gritted her teeth and reminded herself that Lila didn't know the ad was hers. "Don't think of it that way," Jessica said. "Think of it as a good way to sort through your possibilities and avoid picking any jerks." She paused. "In fact, I was thinking about placing an ad myself in next week's edition."

"Really?" Lila asked, looking thoughtful.

"Yes," Jessica said. She figured she was only stretching the truth a tiny bit.

Jessica began to explain how the personal ads worked, still being careful not to give away her se-cret. The more she talked, the more excited Lila be-came.

"Do you really think guys would respond to my ad?" she asked eagerly. "Cute, rich guys?"

"If you make it good," Jessica answered, think-ing of her own responses. Even though none of the guys who had written to her so far had sounded just right, most of them hadn't actually sounded terrible, either—well, except for Donald Zwerdling, maybe.

"But I wouldn't know what to say," Lila said. She thought for a moment. "What about 'Incredibly rich and beautiful princess with expensive tastes and high standards seeks fabulous prince charming to lavish her with attention.'"

"Um . . ." Jessica said. "That sounds a little . . . strong. You don't want to scare anyone."

"Right," Lila said. "How about 'Beautiful brunette seeks hot guy to lavish her with attention and romantic gifts.'"

Jessica wrinkled her nose. "How about 'Material girl seeks material guy'?"

Lila grinned. "I like it! Hey, Jessica, you're pretty good at this. How about helping me write the rest?"

Jessica felt flattered. She *did* seem to have a knack for this sort of thing. "Sure," she said. "If you want."

Lila squeezed her arm. "We'll work on it after lunch, OK? And it'll be our secret. Jake Hamilton, *adios* forever."

Elizabeth sat in her math class, fuming. All around her, her classmates were *still* discussing Jessica's personal ad. Elizabeth couldn't believe it. Didn't people have anything better to think about?

"Hey, Wakefield," Charlie Cashman said, stopping at Elizabeth's desk. "Great work on the *Sixers* this week."

"Thanks a lot," Elizabeth replied grumpily. *Charlie Cashman has probably never read the newspaper in his whole life until now,* she thought. *He must have heard about that stupid personal ad and decided to check it out.*

Charlie didn't seem to notice her mood. "How about telling me the real identity of 'Gorgeous Blonde'?" he said.

"Forget it," she snapped.

He shrugged and grinned. "Hey, it was worth a shot," he said, walking away. "By the way," he added over his shoulder, "I liked your story about the track team. It was pretty cool."

Elizabeth was surprised. Charlie was known to be the class troublemaker, and she wouldn't have expected him to take an interest in any article that appeared in the *Sixers*. She'd never even seen him reading a copy of the paper before. In fact, when she thought about it, she couldn't remember ever seeing him reading *anything* before.

Her thoughts were interrupted by Caroline Pearce, who leaned over and began asking questions about the personal ad, obviously trying to find out who had written it. Elizabeth had always known Caroline was nosy, but she couldn't believe how persistent she could be.

The more time Elizabeth had to spend fending off Caroline's probing questions, the more annoyed she got. When the teacher finally walked into the room to start class, Elizabeth was relieved.

This personal ad business is making my life miserable, she thought angrily. *And it's all Jessica's fault!*

The next afternoon Jessica was on her way to class when she passed her twin in the hallway. "Hi, Elizabeth," she said cheerfully. She was in a good mood because she had received several new responses the day before. Even though none of them had quite sounded like Mr. Right, Jessica was sure she was getting closer.

To her surprise, Elizabeth just gave her a dirty look and hurried past without a word. *That's strange*, thought Jessica. *I wonder what's with her?* But before she could think about it any further she heard Janet Howell calling her from the other end of the hall. She turned around and saw Janet hurrying toward her.

"I have to talk to you," Janet said. She took Jessica by the elbow and dragged her into the girls' bathroom. She carefully checked the stalls to be sure they were alone. "It's extremely confidential. Promise you won't tell a soul."

"Sure." Jessica was pleased that Janet trusted her enough to tell her a secret. After all, Janet was the president of the Unicorns—she could have picked anyone. "What's up?"

"Lila told me how you helped her write a personal ad," Janet whispered.

"She did?" Even though Janet and Lila were

cousins, Jessica was a little surprised that Lila had told Janet about the ad. She had sworn Jessica to secrecy about it.

"I've been thinking about me and Denny lately," Janet went on. "Maybe I should see what else is out there. Think of what I've been missing. All those boys . . . all that fun . . ."

"But you have fun with Denny," Jessica said. "He brings you brownies for lunch."

Janet wrinkled her nose. "Brownies. Big deal. All he ever gives me is food." She frowned. "I was hoping that since you helped Lila write a personal ad, you'd help me too."

Jessica couldn't believe it. Janet wanted *her* to help write her personal ad? "Sure," Jessica agreed, holding back a triumphant grin.

Janet seemed relieved. "Great. You won't tell anyone, will you?"

"Of course not. Nobody will ever know except you and Mr. Right," Jessica assured her. "The ads are anonymous, remember?"

Janet nodded happily. "What should we say? Something about my looks? My good taste? My leadership qualities?"

"All that and more," Jessica said. "Don't worry about a thing, Janet. You're going to find the perfect new boyfriend this way."

Janet gazed into the mirror and played with her hair, a thoughtful smile on her face. "Do you really think so?"

Jessica thought about all the responses that had poured into her box in the last two days. "I know so," she said.

That evening, the Wakefields' dinner table was especially quiet. "Mom, would you ask Jessica to pass the broccoli, please?" Elizabeth said soon after they were seated.

"Hold on. I haven't had any myself yet," Jessica answered breezily.

Elizabeth pretended not to hear her. She dumped a spoonful of rice onto her plate and stabbed at her chicken with her fork. She was furious at Jessica. And the worst part was, she had been giving her twin the silent treatment for two days and Jessica hadn't even noticed!

"How was school today, girls?" Mrs. Wakefield asked.

"Terrific," Jessica said with a sunny smile.

Elizabeth looked up from her plate. "Mom, ask Jessica to pass the salt, please," she said sullenly.

"Ask her yourself," Steven said.

Elizabeth gave him a dirty look.

Mrs. Wakefield cleared her throat. "Elizabeth, is there some reason you can't communicate with Jessica yourself?"

Elizabeth didn't answer.

Mr. Wakefield looked from one twin to the other. "Would someone please tell me what's going on?" he said.

"Beats me," Jessica said, glancing at her sister. "I guess Elizabeth isn't talking to me."

Elizabeth put down her fork and narrowed her eyes. "Do you want to know why?" she asked Jessica evenly.

"Yes," Steven said eagerly.

"Stay out of this, Steven," Mr. Wakefield said warningly.

"Now, Elizabeth," Mrs. Wakefield said soothingly. "What's all this about?"

Elizabeth took a deep breath. "I'm upset because today when I went to check the *Sixers* mailbox it was crammed—and I mean crammed—full of personal ads." She glared at Jessica. "And it's all your fault."

Jessica shrugged. "So your paper's popular. You can thank me later."

"*Thank* you!" Elizabeth cried in disbelief, throwing down her fork. "I should never have let you advertise for a boyfriend in the classified section in the first place! Now, instead of running a newspaper, I'm running a dating service!"

Steven's eyes widened. "You mean, you mean . . ." He leaned forward in his chair and choked back a laugh. "Jessica is actually *advertising* for a boyfriend?" He leaned back and began howling with laughter.

Jessica sat up stiffly. "I happen to have ten responses already." She turned to Elizabeth and shrugged. "Hey, look. I can't help it if it was a good idea."

"I'll say," Steven gasped between guffaws. "Hey, Jess, do you offer a money-back guarantee?" He laughed so hard at that that he fell off his chair onto the floor.

"Steven!" Mrs. Wakefield said sharply. "That's enough!"

"S-s-sorry, Mom," he chortled, holding his stomach as he rolled back and forth on the floor, trying to stop laughing.

Elizabeth wasn't paying any attention to Steven. She was still glaring at Jessica, feeling as if she were about to explode. "How can you say it was a good idea?" she demanded.

"Well, it's working, isn't it?" Jessica said. "The classified service is a hit."

"No, it's not. Your ad is the only thing people are looking at. The classified section is supposed to offer people practical help in finding things they need."

"Like boyfriends," Jessica said.

Elizabeth threw up her arms. "I can't believe you!"

"Hey, don't blame me if people like the idea," Jessica said. "You just can't stand the fact that you were wrong and I was right."

Mrs. Wakefield shook her head. "Jessica, that's not a very nice thing to say."

"OK, sorry," Jessica said with a shrug.

But Elizabeth could tell that Jessica wasn't sorry. Not one bit.

*   *   *

That night Elizabeth lay in bed staring at the ceiling. She had calmed down since dinner, but she still couldn't sleep because she was so worried about the new direction the newspaper was taking. Were her instincts all wrong?

Elizabeth found herself thinking back once again to the *Unicorn News* fiasco several months ago. How did Jessica always seem to know exactly what would sell, what people would want to read, what they were interested in?

Elizabeth rolled over onto her side and stared out the window. She would never in a million years have guessed that personal ads would be this popular. She had been sure people would think they were silly. But Jessica had known better.

Elizabeth rolled over and buried her head in her pillow. As much as she hated to admit it, this time Jessica seemed to have come up with a winner. Elizabeth hadn't seen this kind of interest in the newspaper in a long time. If even Charlie Cashman was complimenting her on the articles, maybe this personal ad business wasn't all bad.

Should she print the personals people had submitted in the next week's issue? She didn't want to. But she knew her classmates would be disappointed if she didn't. Did that obligate her to do it? She didn't think it did. On the other hand, she couldn't help wondering if her ideals were just too high. After all, the *Sixers* wasn't *The New York Times*.

Maybe it was better to include something like the personal ads if it meant more people would pick up the paper. Maybe she should just give in and admit that she had been wrong about Jessica's idea.

She sighed. As much as she hated the whole idea, she reluctantly decided she had to give her readers what they wanted.

Six

◇

"Hi, everybody. I'm home!" Jessica called out as she hurried through the front door the following Monday afternoon. "Anybody here?"

"I'm in here," a voice responded from the kitchen.

Jessica walked into the kitchen. Steven was sitting at the table stuffing his face with potato chips.

"Where's Mom?" Jessica asked, taking a handful of potato chips. "And Elizabeth?"

Steven took a noisy gulp of milk and wiped his face with the back of his hand. "They went to the grocery store," he said, grabbing the bag away from her. "They'll be back later."

"Thanks," Jessica said. *Good!* she thought. She went upstairs to her bedroom and shut the door. She was about to go through another batch of responses and she wanted total privacy.

She settled herself on the bed and pulled the letters out of her backpack.

"Yo, Jessica!" Steven called from downstairs.

She sighed noisily, dropped the letters on her bed, and went out into the hall. "What do you want?" she yelled down the stairs.

"I forgot to tell you. Mom said you were supposed to take out the garbage today. It's your turn, remember?"

Jessica sighed again. "OK." She tramped back downstairs. She hated taking out the garbage. It was smelly and disgusting. As quickly as she could, she dragged the full cans to the curb. "Yuck." She hurried back to her room and closed the door again.

Jessica carefully spread that day's batch of responses out on the bed. Five letters. Not bad.

She unfolded the first one. It was from a boy who started off by announcing that his favorite thing was surfing. "Mmmm," she said, tossing it aside. "I'm not that into surfers."

Number two said he liked rock music and junk food. Jessica was interested. She read on. He described himself as blond and muscular, and said he liked to travel. *Maybe*, she thought. She put his letter into a separate "possible" pile.

The third note was from a boy who loved football and kung fu movies. Jessica shook her head and tossed the paper onto the growing pile of rejects on the floor next to her bed.

At the mention of kung fu movies, though, Jessica was reminded of Mandy's problems with Peter. For a moment, she entertained the uncomfortable thought that response number three might be from Peter. Maybe Jessica's ad was the reason he had broken up with Mandy! No, it couldn't be. Peter wasn't the type to respond to a personal ad. She forced the thought out of her mind.

The fourth response was Donald Zwerdling again. Didn't the poor guy know when to give up?

Jessica picked up the last letter. She didn't remember seeing it before, but she figured it had probably been stuck in among the others. It was neatly folded and carefully typewritten. *Hmmm*, she thought. *Good start.* She began to read: "Dear Gorgeous Blonde," the note said. "I've always hoped to meet someone like you. But finding a girlfriend hasn't been easy for me. You see, even though I'm only in tenth grade (someone left a copy of the *Sixers* with your ad in it lying around the high school library) I'm already a professional studio musician and so most of my spare time is spent jamming and recording with my musician friends. I got started in the music business because of my cousin. His name is Johnny Buck. Maybe you've heard of him."

Jessica gasped. No way! Johnny Buck's cousin? It sounded too good to be true! Quickly, she read on: "Anyway, being around rock stars all the time can be exciting but lonely. I'd like to be able to take someone like you with me to recording sessions and concerts, and on our days off we could relax at the beach or go shopping. By the way, I can hardly wait until next month when I turn sixteen and get my driver's license. I've already saved up enough money to buy a Porsche."

Jessica stopped for a moment. She couldn't believe her good luck. A musician with money and fame? Even Lila couldn't top this one! Lila was going to die of jealousy!

But there had to be a catch. Why hadn't this guy already found a girlfriend? Maybe he was funny-looking or something. Still, he did have a lot of other things going for him. For Johnny Buck's rich, famous cousin she might be able to overlook a big nose or buckteeth.

Jessica glanced down at the letter again. It was signed "Rock Lives." She noticed a P.S. "I have some free time tomorrow afternoon. If you're interested in meeting me, I'll be at the Dairi Burger around 4 o'clock. I'll be the one wearing a *Rolling Rocks* magazine T-shirt and a "Boys Next Door" baseball cap. Later, Gorgeous."

Jessica sighed and threw herself back on her pillow, clutching the note to her heart. *This could be the guy,* she thought, a smile forming on her face. She pictured herself sitting in on one of Johnny Buck's studio sessions. *That would be so great!* she thought. Then she pictured how jealous the Unicorns would be when they found out about her new boyfriend. She grinned. *That would be even better!* She could just picture them, begging her for backstage passes. She'd probably be able to get a lot of free CDs and posters, too.

She didn't want to get too excited, though. Just to be sure, she'd go to the Dairi Burger and take a look at him first. That way she couldn't lose. If he was weird or anything, she could just leave. After all, he wouldn't know who she was.

She folded up the letter and carefully put it in her drawer. She could hardly wait until the next afternoon.

Jessica spent the following day in a blur. She couldn't concentrate on anything anybody said to her. She couldn't even eat lunch because she was so busy thinking about "Rock Lives." Who *was* this guy? Why hadn't she ever heard of him before? She couldn't wait to check him out.

After school she rushed home to change. She slipped into a pair of black jeans, her brand-new black vest, and her favorite pair of dangling silver earrings. She studied herself in the mirror. Perfect. She thought she looked just like a girl who would hang around with famous rock musicians.

The Dairi Burger was only a short walk from the Wakefields' house, but Jessica didn't usually go there, since it was more of a high school hangout. When she reached the restaurant, she took a deep breath, walked up to the front door, and pushed it open. Inside, the place was packed. Jessica scanned the crowd. She noticed one of Steven's ninth-grade friends, Chad Lucas, sitting with a group of guys in a booth near the front of the room.

"Hi, Jessica," he called, waving at her. "You look great today."

Jessica blushed. "Oh, hi, Chad," she said, waving back. For a second she felt flustered. She wasn't really used to getting compliments from high school boys—and Chad *was* awfully cute. In fact, she had had a big crush on him once. Still, she reminded herself, she had to remember to act mature. "Rock Lives" would definitely not be impressed if she acted like a babyish sixth grader.

Jessica looked around carefully. Even though a lot of kids were wearing baseball caps, none of the hats said "Boys Next Door" on them.

She started searching the tables, one by one. Nothing. Where was he? Had he changed his mind?

Then, in the far corner of the room, she noticed someone sitting alone with his back toward her. He had on a baseball cap. Backwards.

Jessica was too far away to read the lettering on the cap, especially since it was sort of dark back there in the corner. Her heart pounding, she moved closer to get a better look.

When she was three tables away, Jessica stopped. She caught her breath. His hat said, "Boys Next Door." Her eyes moved down to his T-shirt. . . . ROLLING ROCKS 20TH ANNIVERSARY, said the lettering on the back. It was him!

Jessica moved closer. She wanted to see his face, but it was impossible. He was hunched over against the wall, reading a copy of *Guitar Stars* magazine.

Poor guy, she thought. *He's all alone. Probably just waiting for me, hoping I'll show up.*

By now she was almost at his table, and still she had no clue what he looked like. What was she supposed to do? If she was ever going to meet him, she'd just have to take a chance and introduce herself. She had no other choice.

She took a deep breath, smoothed her hair, and moved another step closer. From the back he didn't look bad. She stepped up to the table. He was still hunched over with his back to her, reading. She cleared her throat nervously. "Excuse me," she said. He didn't look up.

"Excuse me," Jessica said again, louder. "Are you Rock Lives?"

He turned around slowly.

Jessica gasped.

A horribly disfigured face stared back at her. He had no mouth, just a gaping hole. No eyes, just dark sockets. And skin that looked like elephant leather. "That's me, Gorgeous," he said in a high, quavering voice. He let out a frightening cackle and reached out for her.

Jessica screamed. Loudly. She turned to run.

"No, Jessica, wait!" the guy called.

Jessica spun back around. *How did he know her*

name? Her heart was pounding. "Who are you?" she demanded.

Rock Lives stood up and peeled off his face. For a second Jessica was on the verge of screaming again, but then she realized it was a mask. An ugly rubber mask. And underneath the mask was the very real face of Steven Wakefield, and *that* face was now laughing hysterically.

"Steven," she gasped. "You jerk! You toad! You moron!"

Jessica looked around. She realized that practically everyone in the Dairi Burger was laughing at her. But no one was laughing harder than Steven.

"I can't believe you fell for that," he said, clutching his sides, gasping for breath. "I stuck that letter on your bed with the others yesterday when you went to take out the garbage. And you totally fell for it!" He went into another fit of laughter. "You should have seen the look on your face!"

"Very funny," Jessica said stiffly. She tried to stay calm, even though what she really wanted was to leap at her brother and strangle him with her bare hands.

"You are so gullible," Steven said, wiping tears from the corners of his eyes. He tossed the hat and mask over to Chad Lucas, who had strolled over and was grinning at them. "Thanks for the loan, Chad. And for warning me when Clueless Blonde here was coming."

"Any time," Chad said. He smiled at Jessica. "I

hope Steven didn't scare you too much. He promised he'd go easy."

"Yeah," Jessica squeaked, knowing her face had turned bright red. "You are such a snake," she hissed at Steven under her breath. "I'll get you back for this. You just wait."

Steven laughed. "What are you going to do? Get all your new boyfriends to beat me up?"

Jessica tossed her head and stalked out of the Dairi Burger without another word. In the future, she told herself, she'd be more careful about the ads she answered. A lot more careful.

That night Jessica sat in her room, feeling discouraged. Rick Hunter's party was coming up in less than two weeks, and she still didn't have a date. Steven's little joke that afternoon had just made that all the more obvious.

Spread out on her bed in front of her were all the responses she'd received so far. She had decided to go through the pile again and examine each one more thoroughly. Maybe she'd overlooked someone, not given him the chance he deserved.

Jessica leaned over and grabbed an empty shoe box off the top of a stack of overdue library books. If she was going to do this right, she was going to have to get organized.

She ripped the box lid in half and used the pieces of cardboard as partitions, creating three sections in the box. Then on three separate index cards she wrote the following signs: NOT IF HE WERE THE LAST GUY ON EARTH for the first section, MORE FUN THAN A TOOTHACHE for the second. She thought for a second. THE LOVE OF MY LIFE, she wrote with a flourish for the third.

Jessica placed one card in each of the three sections in the box. Then she started going through her pile of responses one by one. Some of them, like the ones from Donald Zwerdling, were easy to decide. Others were tougher. Jessica gave each letter her most careful consideration, first trying to decide whether she thought it was another joke.

It was past eleven when Jessica finally finished. Exhausted, she reviewed her findings. The second and third slots were full, crammed to the top.

The first slot, though, the LOVE OF MY LIFE slot, was still empty.

Jessica shoved the shoe box under her bed, stretched, and sighed. Finding the perfect guy wasn't going to be easy, especially since she didn't have much time before the party.

For a moment she thought wistfully of Aaron. Things would be much simpler if she were still going to the party with him. Then she pushed that thought to the back of her mind. Aaron was out of the picture, and she was glad. She was going to find her perfect match through the personals—she was sure of it. It was just going to take a little longer than she'd thought.

Seven

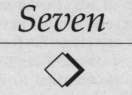

Elizabeth was sitting in the *Sixers* office after lunch, trying her best to concentrate on the article she was supposed to be writing. It was a profile on the new student teacher, Mr. Rosensohn. He'd been a news reporter before he'd decided to switch to teaching. Even though she was interested in her subject, it wasn't easy to concentrate on what she was doing. All morning long, people had been flocking to the office to check their response boxes.

She picked up the latest edition of the *Sixers* and sighed. It contained four pages of news and six pages of personals. She'd printed extra copies of this week's edition, but practically every single one was already gone, even though the paper had only come out that morning. Even seventh and eighth graders were grabbing them up. Where would it all end?

"Hi, Elizabeth." Sophia Rizzo came into the office and went directly to a response box.

"Hi, Sophia," Elizabeth said. She wasn't even shocked anymore that couples like Sophia Rizzo and Patrick Morris or Belinda Layton and Jim Sturbridge were all advertising in the personals. It seemed that everyone wanted in on the action, even couples that had been together for a long time.

Sophia left and two eighth-grade boys came in. "Nothing yet," one reported to the other. "Maybe later." They walked back out.

Elizabeth shook her head. Who would have thought that even the eighth graders would be so interested in personals? She would have thought that by eighth grade they would have more important things to think about.

Just then Amy walked in. "Oh, hi," Elizabeth greeted her. "I'm so glad it's you. I'm having a terrible time concentrating, thanks to these dumb response boxes."

Amy must not have heard her. She marched right past Elizabeth and straight to one of the response boxes. She stuck her hand inside it and felt around. "Darn," she said. "No luck yet."

Elizabeth gasped. Were her eyes tricking her or had she just seen Amy—her best friend, one of the most sensible and logical people she knew—checking a response box? "Amy!" she exclaimed. "What are you doing?"

Amy turned around. "What does it look like?"

Elizabeth's eyes grew wide. "*You* ran a personal ad?"

Amy gave her a slightly embarrassed smile. "Well, I guess I changed my mind."

Elizabeth couldn't believe it. "What do you mean you changed your mind? Amy, how could you *do* something like this?"

Amy shrugged. "It's only for fun," she said defensively. "It's not a big deal."

"Not a big deal!" Elizabeth cried. "But what about everything you were saying about the standards of the paper? Being taken seriously as a source of real news? Can't you see that by supporting this ridiculous personals craze you're just hurting everything we've worked to accomplish with the *Sixers*?"

"Lighten up, Elizabeth," Amy said with a frown. "I admit I had my doubts about personal ads at first, but it's all just for fun. I think Jessica really hit on something great with this idea."

Elizabeth couldn't believe her ears. She felt hurt and betrayed—she never would have expected Amy to act like this! "Well, if you think Jessica has such great ideas," Elizabeth said angrily, "maybe *she* should be the editor of the *Sixers* instead of me." She grabbed her books and stormed out of the office, leaving Amy staring after her in astonishment.

At the other end of the school, Jessica was hurrying to study hall, clutching the latest edition of the *Sixers* under her arm. All day she'd been waiting for the right moment to go through it. Now she'd have an entire class period to browse at her own pace.

When she reached the classroom, Jessica settled into an out-of-the-way spot in the corner and spread the paper out on her desk. Maybe this was her chance to find something better than what she'd already received. She planned to sit there until she'd read every ad on all six pages.

She quickly flipped through the first four pages of the paper, which were just boring news stories. Then the personals started.

Jessica couldn't believe how many people had run ads. She took out a pencil and began slowly going down the first column. A lot of the ads were girls looking for guys. She noticed Lila's ad and smiled. Then the one just below caught her eye. "Athletic guy seeks fun-loving girlfriend. Likes faded Levi's, Johnny Buck, haunted houses, and pineapple pizza. Hates electric toothbrushes, movies with subtitles, diet anything. Respond to Box #23."

Jessica's heart skipped a beat. Someone else out there loved pineapple pizza? She had thought she was the only one. In fact, she had pretty much given up trying to talk people into ordering it. Now she usually only ate it on her birthday, when her father always bought her a whole pizza for herself.

She circled the ad and put a big star beside it before moving on to the next ad. But as she read, her eyes kept straying back to the ad from Athletic Guy. He sounded so . . . perfect. She tried not to get her hopes up too much, though. She'd learned her lesson with Steven.

When she had gone through every ad, she went back and carefully tore out Athletic Guy's ad. She had noticed the study hall monitor giving her dirty looks the whole time she'd been reading the newspaper, so she decided she'd better at least pretend to study for the rest of the period. Today of all days she didn't want to be stuck in detention—not when she could be home composing the perfect response to Athletic Guy's ad.

She opened her science textbook and stuck the personal ad on top of a diagram of a water molecule. That way she would be able to stare at it and try to think of the best way to write back.

By the time the bell rang, Jessica had Athletic Guy's ad memorized. She grabbed her things and headed into the hall, where she ran into Lila.

"Jessica!" Lila squealed. She breathlessly pulled Jessica into the nearest corner. "Jessica, I just wanted to thank you for helping me write that ad. I've already had three responses." She glanced around, lowered her voice, and added smugly, "Janet's only had two."

"Congratulations," Jessica said. "I told you your ad was a killer. Anything good so far?"

Lila shrugged. "Nothing bad, but nothing quite

right." She tossed her head. "After all, I think I have a right to be pretty choosy. I don't want to end up with another Jake." She frowned for a moment, but then her smile returned. "Anyway, if I've had this many responses already, who knows how many guys I'll have to choose from before the party!" Her eyes gleamed at the thought. "How about you? You said you were going to place an ad. Any luck?"

"Maybe," Jessica said, thinking of Athletic Guy. She didn't want to tell Lila about him until she was sure he was as perfect as he sounded.

Lila waved to Belinda Layton, who was across the hall. "Did I tell you Belinda decided to run a personal ad, too? She said she wants to expand her horizons. All she and Jim ever talk about is sports." Lila squeezed Jessica's arm. "Isn't this great? I have to hand it to you, Jessica. It looks as though you've started a new fad. I can't wait to hear if Belinda's had any luck so far." Lila hurried off to talk to Belinda.

"'Bye," Jessica said. She glanced down at the ad from Athletic Guy again and smiled. Maybe this was everyone's lucky day.

That night, Jessica couldn't sleep. All she could think about was Athletic Guy's ad. He sounded so different from the guys who had responded to her ad. Better. More fun. She slowly went over the list of things he liked again. Pineapple pizza, faded Levi's, Johnny Buck, haunted houses . . .

Jessica smiled and tried to picture him. If he liked haunted houses, she bet he liked roller coasters, too. And loud rock music. He sounded like a thrill seeker, just like her. And he must be a cool dresser if he liked faded Levi's.

Jessica got out of bed and went over to her desk. She turned on the lamp and began shuffling through her bottom drawer.

"Aha!" she said. She pulled out a slightly smashed pink stationery box and gently pried off the lid. Inside were several sheets of rose-scented paper.

Jessica took out the top piece and smoothed it with her hand. It took a few more minutes of rummaging to locate a pen that worked. Finally she was ready.

She chewed on the pen for a moment, then began writing. "Dear Athletic Guy, Your ad sounded interesting, especially the pizza part. . . ." She frowned. Nah. Too boring. Athletic Guy was fun and adventurous. She had to make sure to sound that way, too, if she wanted to get his attention.

She took out another piece of stationery and tried again. "Dear Athletic Guy, Wow! I thought I was the only person in the world who liked pineapple pizza!"

Better, she thought.

She continued. "What else do you like? If we're as much alike as I think, I'll bet you like roller coasters (especially the ones with loops), horror movies (ones with lots of sequels), and strawberry Pop-Tarts with icing. I hope I'm right."

Jessica signed the letter Gorgeous Blonde, carefully put it into a clean pink envelope, and neatly sealed it shut. Across the front she wrote "Box #23" and underlined it with a flourish.

There! If that didn't get a response from Athletic Guy, then nothing would, she thought with satisfaction.

She tucked the envelope into her backpack and crawled back into bed. This time she fell asleep quickly, and dreamed about cute boys, roller coasters, and pineapple pizza all night long.

Eight

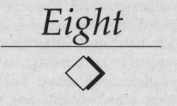

Elizabeth sat in the *Sixers* office, trying her best to concentrate. Two days had passed since the paper had come out, and still the office was bustling with people coming to check their response boxes.

She forced her eyes back to the computer screen to reread what she'd written. "Sweet Valley Middle School is getting a new computer system," she read. "The new system will be able to link all the school's computers together, including those serving the library."

She was interrupted again, this time by Tamara Chase, who pulled a note from her box and screamed. "He wrote back! I don't believe it."

"Congratulations," Elizabeth said dryly. She was actually starting to get used to the personals fever that had swept the middle school. Sort of. The only problem was, she still hadn't made up with Amy. They hadn't spoken since their fight the other day. Elizabeth felt bad about yelling at her friend. When she had calmed down and thought it over, she realized she didn't have any right telling Amy she couldn't run a personal ad. Especially since Amy's sort-of boyfriend, Ken Matthews, didn't seem to mind a bit. He had been in to check his own response box several times already that day.

Elizabeth sighed and stared at the screen. The computer article was actually one that Amy was supposed to write. But Elizabeth wasn't sure Amy would even want to write for the *Sixers* anymore, especially now when she was so busy finding a new boyfriend.

"Hi, Elizabeth," a voice interrupted her thoughts.

Elizabeth looked up, and her heart sank. It was Todd Wilkins, her boyfriend. She and Todd had liked each other for a long time, but he didn't usually stop in to see her in the *Sixers* office. Could that mean . . . ? *Oh, no.* She couldn't help but suspect the worst.

"Hi, Todd," she said glumly. "I guess you're here to check a response box."

Todd looked shocked. "Elizabeth! Why would I want to do that?"

Elizabeth shrugged. "I don't know, but everybody else does."

"I don't need to find a girlfriend," he said, smiling at her a little sheepishly. "I already know the most perfect girl in the world."

Elizabeth felt the blood rush to her cheeks. How could she have doubted Todd? He was so incredibly sweet.

Todd pulled up a chair beside Elizabeth and sat down. "I actually came to ask you if you wanted to go to Rick Hunter's party with me."

"Oh!" Elizabeth caught her breath. "I'd love to!" She shook her head. "I'm sorry I accused you of taking out a personal ad. I just . . ." She felt awful.

"That's OK." He looked at her more closely. "Are you all right, Elizabeth? You've seemed kind of preoccupied the last few days."

"I know. It's just that I can't believe how well Jessica's idea is working."

"What idea?"

"This whole personals craze started because of Jessica," Elizabeth explained. "She's the one who started the ads, and now it seems like every couple in school is breaking up and advertising for someone else. Even couples I thought were perfectly happy—Amy and Ken, Mandy Miller and Peter Jeffries, Sophia Rizzo and Patrick Morris—"

"But not us," Todd interrupted her.

Elizabeth blushed again. "Yeah, I know. I'm glad about that."

"Besides," Todd continued, "hasn't the paper been getting lots of extra attention because of the personals?"

Elizabeth frowned. "Sure it has. But that has absolutely nothing to do with the news. Everyone just wants to read the personals. It's pretty depressing. Maybe I should forget about the news altogether and just run personals. It'd be a lot more popular." She sat back and sighed.

Todd nodded sympathetically. "Listen, maybe it's not all as bad as you think. Maybe some of the people who pick up the *Sixers* to read the personals also read some of the other articles, too. You never know."

Elizabeth remembered Charlie Cashman's compliments. "Yeah, I guess. Still, I can't help hoping this fad ends soon."

"It will," Todd said. "In the meantime, you should just try to enjoy the extra attention the paper is getting." He laughed. "It's too bad you don't charge money for the newspapers. Think how rich you'd be right now."

Elizabeth looked at Todd and blinked. "Omigod! That's it!" she exclaimed.

"What?"

"You just gave me the best idea! We don't charge for papers, but we *could* charge for personals."

Todd looked thoughtful. "I guess you could. Why not? After all, regular newspapers always charge for classifieds."

Elizabeth grew even more excited. "Hey! Maybe my idea about forgetting the news and just running personal ads isn't so bad. We could run a special personals edition," she said. "We'll charge a dollar an ad."

"A bargain," Todd said, grinning. "I'd do it."

Elizabeth's face fell.

"Just kidding," he said with a grin.

"Very funny," Elizabeth said, grinning too. She jumped to her feet. "I'd better go find Mr. Bowman to ask his permission. I hope he says yes."

"What'll you do with all the money you make?" Todd asked, standing up as well.

"I don't know," Elizabeth said. "I guess the newspaper staff could vote on it. It doesn't matter, we'll come up with something good." She grabbed Todd's hand. "Thanks for the idea," she told him. She stopped in the doorway. "And thanks for not looking for a new girlfriend."

Jessica almost collided with her twin as Elizabeth came rushing out of the *Sixers* office.

"Oh, hi, Lizzie," Jessica said.

To her surprise, Elizabeth gave her a huge smile. "Hi, Jess! How's it going?"

"Uh, OK," Jessica said. What had happened to Elizabeth? The twins had hardly spoken a word to each other for the past two weeks, and now Elizabeth was acting as though nothing had ever come between them. "How come you look so excited?" she asked.

"Todd just had the best idea," Elizabeth said. "The paper's going to sponsor a special personals edition. We'll charge a dollar an ad."

"Sounds good," Jessica said. She peeked around Elizabeth to check her response box. No luck.

"I think it's going to be a big hit," Elizabeth said. "Don't you?"

"Probably," Jessica said. She moved slightly to the right and peered through the office door. She was dying to check her response box. She'd had her fingers crossed all day, hoping Athletic Guy would write back. "Listen, Lizzie. I'm really sorry, but I have to go."

Elizabeth didn't even seem offended. "Me too. I'll see you later, OK?"

"OK," Jessica said. She hurried into the office. Todd was the only one there. "Hi, Todd."

"Hi, Jessica," Todd replied. "What's up?"

"Nothing much," Jessica said, hoping he would leave so she could check her box in private.

"I'll see you around," Todd said. "I've got to get to basketball practice."

Jessica smiled sweetly as he headed for the door. As soon as he was out of sight, she dove for her response box. There were two letters inside it. She opened the first one and quickly skimmed its contents. "Dear Gorgeous Blonde, I saw your ad last week and wanted to write back but was out sick until now. . . ."

"Nah," she said, stuffing it into her backpack.

The second letter she didn't even bother to read once she saw the signature. It was from someone who called himself "Magic Man," and whether he was magic or not, Jessica didn't care. All she cared about was a letter from Athletic Guy—and that letter still hadn't come.

Jessica sighed heavily. Why hadn't she heard from him? It had been two days now. She thought back to his ad, then to her letter. Hadn't he liked what she'd written? Had he gotten lots of other responses he liked better? She felt like crying when she thought of that. He'd sounded so perfect for her.

Jessica glanced at the wall clock. It was time for Boosters practice. She could check again when it was over. Maybe by then there'd be a response.

When Jessica arrived in the gym, she was surprised to see Amy, Lila, Mandy, and Janet clustered together, giggling. *That's weird,* she thought. Except for Winston Egbert, Amy was the only member of the Boosters cheering squad who wasn't a Unicorn. Normally Amy didn't spend much time gossiping and giggling with the other Boosters before practice.

Curious, Jessica walked up to the group. "What's so funny?" she asked.

"Donald Zwerdling wrote us all the same form letter," Mandy said with a laugh. "He has some nerve, doesn't he?"

Jessica laughed, too. "Did it start off with a poem?"

"Yes!" they chorused.

"I got one, too," Jessica said. "Well, actually, I've gotten three letters from him. But the first one was the one with the poem. Someone should tell him he'd have better luck if he went anonymous."

Everyone laughed. "I think the whole idea of having these personal ads is great," Janet announced. "I'm getting tons of great responses. This guy called Lonely Biker seems especially promising. He's written to me three times already."

"Really?" Jessica said. "What's he like?" Usually Janet was really picky about whom she liked. Jessica was surprised she'd found someone so quickly.

"He sounds wonderful," Janet said. "He says he's athletic and funny, and he's dying to meet me in person."

"I think the personals are great, too," Lila said. She grabbed Jessica's hands. "You won't believe it, Jessica. I think I've found somebody I really like."

"Really?"

Lila nodded. "He signed his letter Beach Bum. At first the 'Bum' part turned me off, but then I realized it didn't matter. I have enough money for both of us."

"That's a very noble attitude, Lila," Amy said dryly.

Lila ignored Amy's comment. "Anyway, I wrote him back and now he's written to me again." She tossed her hair. "I think he's crazy about me already. And when he meets me in person, he'll be even more impressed."

"That's great," Jessica said, trying not to feel envious. She thought about Athletic Guy's lack of response and frowned a little. "I'm happy for you."

"I'm writing to someone, too," Kimberly Haver said. "He's called Cool Rebel."

"What a great name!" Janet exclaimed.

"I know," Kimberly replied. "And he sounds just as great as his name, too."

"Isn't it fun?" Amy said. "The guy I'm writing to, Rock Jock, is so goofy. He sends me little presents through my response box, like bags of potato chips and gummy worms. I love gummy worms."

"Wow," Jessica said. "He didn't say anything about . . . pineapple pizza, did he?"

"*Pineapple* pizza?" Amy rolled her eyes. "I hope not. That sounds really gross."

"Good," Jessica said. Amy gave her a strange look. "By the way, I just saw Elizabeth," Jessica said, changing the subject. "She told me she plans to run a special personals section for the paper. Placing an ad will cost a dollar."

"Really?" Amy said. "That's the first I've heard about it."

"I think she just got the idea," Jessica said.

"Well, I think it's a great idea," Janet said, cutting in. "This is something all the Unicorns should get in on. I'll bring it up at our meeting tomorrow."

"I'm definitely going to run my ad again," Kimberly said.

"What about Cool Rebel?" Jessica asked. "I thought he was the guy of your dreams."

"You never know," Kimberly said. "There might be someone else out there, too. That's what's so fun about these ads. Since everyone's doing it, there's tons of people to choose from."

Right, thought Jessica. It was fun if you found

what you wanted. But what about her? The one person she wanted to hear from obviously wasn't interested in writing to her.

"Is something wrong, Jessica?" Janet asked.

"No," she replied sullenly. It just didn't seem fair. The personal ads had been her idea in the first place. So why did it seem like everyone had hooked up with the perfect new partner except for her?

Elizabeth was back at the *Sixers* office later that afternoon, putting the finishing touches on the computer article, when Amy walked in.

"Hi. What are you working on?" Amy asked, peering over Elizabeth's shoulder.

Elizabeth glanced up, surprised to see her. "The article about the school's new computer system," she said slowly. She wondered if Amy had come to make up.

"The computer article?" Amy said. "But I was planning to write that this weekend."

"Oh, well, I wasn't sure if you still wanted to do it, so I did it for you," Elizabeth said quietly. "Anyway, it's finished now. So you don't have to worry about it." She noticed that Amy was dressed in loose shorts and a big T-shirt. "Did you come from Boosters practice?"

Amy nodded. "We just finished."

There was an awkward silence. Elizabeth wanted to apologize for snapping at Amy about the personal ads, but she didn't know how to begin.

"I'm sorry we had a fight," Amy said at last. "I

never meant to hurt your feelings. I still think the idea of personal ads is kind of silly, but when I saw how much fun people were having, I didn't see anything wrong with joining in."

Elizabeth smiled, relieved. "I know. I'm sorry, too. I overreacted. Jessica had a great idea, and you had every right to try it out." She stood up and hugged Amy. "I'm sorry about the things I said to you the other day."

"That's OK," Amy said, hugging her back. Then they both sat down near the computer. "I hear you had a pretty great idea of your own," Amy said. "Jessica told me we're running a special personals edition."

Elizabeth nodded. "That's right, although actually Todd gave me the idea," she said. "I got permission from Mr. Bowman to charge a dollar an ad. I think it'll be a big moneymaker."

"I do, too. When does it come out?"

"I was thinking about Tuesday, a day ahead of the regular paper, so it won't have to compete with the news," Elizabeth said.

"Since we both know who would win that competition," Amy said wryly. They both laughed. "This is Thursday," Amy said. "That doesn't give us much time." She glanced at the clock. "If we hurry, we can put together an announcement that we can send home with kids tomorrow. Then over the weekend we can put more flyers in the usual spots, like Casey's, the Dairi

Burger, and maybe the record store at the mall."

Elizabeth grabbed a sheet of scrap paper. She was happy that she and Amy were friends again. She realized that as much as she loved working on the *Sixers*, it wouldn't be nearly as much fun without Amy. "Good idea. Let's get started. What should we say?"

"Let's draw a big heart and put the information inside that," Amy suggested. "That should help get people's attention."

"Right," Elizabeth said. She drew the heart. "Now, what should we say inside the heart?"

They both thought for a moment. "I know," Amy said. "How about, 'Get personal with the *Sixers*.'"

"Perfect," Elizabeth said.

By working together, they had the announcement finished in no time. "Now to the photocopy machine," Elizabeth said.

Just then Jessica hurried into the office. "Oh, hi, Elizabeth, you're still here. Anything new come in for me in the last hour or so?"

Elizabeth rolled her eyes at Amy and giggled. "No, Jessica," she said. "No one's been here."

"Oh," Jessica said. She paused. "Are you sure?"

"Positive," Elizabeth said. "I haven't moved from this chair."

Jessica's shoulders slumped. "OK. Well, I'll see you at home." Her shoulders were drooping as she left the room.

Nine

Elizabeth and Amy spent most of the weekend working on advertising the personals edition. On Saturday they got Maria Slater and Sophia Rizzo to help them plaster the mall with flyers. On Sunday afternoon the four of them taped up notices in all the popular local restaurants, including Casey's and the Dairi Burger.

By Monday afternoon things were crazy in the *Sixers* office.

"Wow," Elizabeth said. She was recounting the stack of ads that had come in since that morning. "Does one hundred eighty-seven sound right to you guys?"

Across the table from Elizabeth sat Julie Porter, Sophia, and Amy. "That's what I counted," Julie said, waving a fistful of dollar bills.

Sophia and Amy were hunched over the computer screen. "OK, it's all set up," Amy announced. "If we fit about ten ads per page, that's eighteen pages." She reached across the table and took the stack of ads from Elizabeth. "Sophia, you read and I'll type, OK?"

Sophia nodded.

Elizabeth grinned. All day the office had been flooded with people dropping off ads. Not in her wildest dreams would she have thought her idea would be *this* successful! Originally, she had thought the *Sixers* staff could use the money they made from the personals edition to buy some equipment for the office—a new stapler, some extra rulers—with maybe enough left over to pay for a staff pizza party. But now she realized that they were making some serious money. They would be able to afford something much better.

Tamara Chase and Betsy Gordon rushed into the office, clutching sheets of paper. "Are we too late to drop off our ads?" asked Tamara breathlessly.

"Nope," Elizabeth said, taking their ads and their money. She glanced at the clock. Would Amy and Sophia be able to finish in time? After all, they only had an hour. "Maybe we should find Mary Wallace," she suggested. "She's the fastest typist I know."

"That sounds like a brilliant idea to me," Amy said with relief, sitting back from the keyboard and flexing her fingers. "Get Mary in here."

Luckily, Mary was in study hall, and only too

happy to help out. And even with people continuing to drop off ads right up to the deadline, she was able to get everything typed up before the final bell rang.

In the end they had almost two hundred ads. "This is unbelievable," Elizabeth said, poring over the final copy. "I can't believe so many people placed ads."

"It's pretty amazing," Mary agreed.

Elizabeth looked up. "Your typing is pretty amazing, too. Thanks for the help."

"Anytime," Mary said. "Do you need anything else?"

"I don't think so," Elizabeth said. "Amy and I can take the final copy down to the photocopy machine and run it off." She looked at Sophia and Julie. "Can you come back in a while and help us distribute these?"

"Sure," Julie said. "In the meantime, I guess we should start clearing off these shelves to make space for all the response boxes we're going to have."

Elizabeth's eyes widened. "I didn't even think of that," she said with a giggle, glancing at the shelves that lined the walls of the office. "It's going to look like a shoe store in here pretty soon."

"Don't worry," Sophia said. "We already discussed it with Mr. Bowman. He said we can store the books and things from the shelves in his classroom until this is all over."

"Great," Elizabeth said with a smile. "Thanks for taking care of that, you guys." She and Amy headed for the office to run off copies of the paper.

Halfway there they were intercepted by Jessica. "Stop," she yelled, coming up behind them in the hall. She looked awful, as though she'd just heard some terrible news.

Immediately, Elizabeth became concerned. "What's wrong?"

Jessica's eyes fell on the final copy, which Elizabeth was holding. "Is that the special edition?" she asked.

Elizabeth nodded proudly. "We just finished it. We got such a big response we weren't sure we'd be able to get it all typed up in time, but we did it, thanks to Mary."

"Yeah, yeah, that's great," Jessica said impatiently. "Can I see it?" She sounded desperate.

"Not right now," Elizabeth said. "We're in a hurry. We have to get it run off before the office closes."

"Please?" Jessica begged, wringing her hands and giving her twin a pathetic look. "I can't wait."

Elizabeth looked at Amy, who shrugged. *What's the matter with Jessica?* Elizabeth wondered. Now that she thought about it, Jessica had been acting strange all weekend. She hadn't seemed interested in doing anything except moping around the house. Elizabeth had been too busy distributing the flyers announcing the special edition to pay much attention, but now she wondered if something was really wrong. "Jessica, what's going on?"

Jessica glanced at Amy. "Well, um . . ." she began.

"I can take a hint," Amy said. She took the paper from Elizabeth's hand. "I'll go get started on making the copies while you two talk."

"Thanks, Amy," Jessica said gratefully.

When Amy was gone, Elizabeth turned to her twin. "All right, out with it. What's up?"

Jessica took a deep breath. It was hard for her to admit what was bothering her, even to her sister. "I'm waiting to hear from somebody," she said quietly. "I responded to his personal ad last week and I haven't heard anything."

"Oh, is that all?" Elizabeth said. "Thank goodness. I thought it was something serious."

"This is serious!" Jessica exclaimed. She gulped. "Lizzie, do you think I'm . . . I'm . . . losing my appeal to guys?" She held her breath, almost afraid to hear her sister's answer. The question had been plaguing her all weekend. After all, she had never had any trouble attracting plenty of interested guys—before Athletic Guy, that is.

Elizabeth burst out laughing. When she saw the annoyed look on Jessica's face, she tried to control herself. "Jessica!" she gasped at last. "Is that really what's got you all upset? But that's ridiculous! This guy has never even met you, remember?"

"Well, that's true," Jessica said. "But still, why didn't he like my note?"

"Maybe he doesn't think you two have anything in common," Elizabeth suggested.

Jessica shook her head. "No way. Lizzie, we have everything in common. We're perfect for each other!" She let out a sigh. "So why can't he see that? Why hasn't he written back?"

"Jess, this isn't like you," Elizabeth said. "You don't usually let yourself get so worked up over guys. I haven't seen you this way since you first started liking Aaron."

"Forget about Aaron," Jessica said with a scowl. "He's old news. The only guy I care about right now is Athletic Guy. And he doesn't seem to care about me."

Elizabeth shrugged. "You win some, you lose some," she said philosophically.

"Elizabeth, please. You've got to let me look at the paper," Jessica said. "I have to see if his ad is in there again."

"It's eighteen pages long," Elizabeth replied a little impatiently. "It takes a very long time to read. Besides, you'll be able to see it first thing tomorrow along with everyone else."

Jessica gave her another pathetic look. "Pretty please? For me, your one and only twin sister and best friend in the whole wide world? *Please?*"

Elizabeth sighed. "OK. I'll tell you what. If you want to wait outside the office while we're working, we'll give you the first copy as soon as it's finished."

Jessica gratefully clutched her arm. "Oh, thank you, Lizzie," she said. "I'll never forget this favor as long as I live. Never."

Elizabeth laughed. "Yeah, sure, Jess," she said. "What are best-friend-in-the-whole-wide-world twin sisters for?" She hurried toward the office to help Amy, with Jessica right behind her.

Thirty minutes later Jessica stood outside the office, tapping her foot impatiently. What was taking Elizabeth and Amy so long?

Frustrated, she pushed open the door to the office and stuck her head inside the room. Elizabeth and Amy looked up. "How much longer?" she asked.

Elizabeth groaned. "Jessica! That's about the fifth time you've interrupted us. I told you, we'll give you the first copy as soon as it's all assembled."

"Sorry," Jessica muttered. She slammed the door shut. It wasn't fair, she thought. Didn't being the editor's sister carry some weight? Why couldn't Elizabeth just give her the parts that were already printed? So what if it wasn't already collated?

Jessica sighed and slid down to sit cross-legged on the floor. While she waited, she daydreamed about Athletic Guy.

They were inside a giant white limousine on their way to a Johnny Buck concert. The limo had purple leather upholstery and a TV tuned to a music video channel. There was also a small refrigerator stocked with sodas, mini heart-shaped chocolate bars wrapped in gold foil, and tons of packages of grape bubble gum.

As they rode along, Athletic Guy spread a white tablecloth between them on the back seat and then from the front seat produced a giant pineapple pizza. "You shouldn't have," Jessica said, helping herself to a piece.

"Oh, yes I should," Athletic Guy said.

While they ate their pizza, they listened to Johnny Buck albums and watched music videos with the sound turned off. When they arrived at the concert arena, the limo driver drove them through a side entrance marked "VIP parking."

"Wow," Jessica said. "Who's the VIP?"

"You are," Athletic Guy said, squeezing her hand.

Their car pulled up to the backstage entrance. A cool-looking woman wearing a leopard-print bodysuit met them there. "Follow me," she said with a smile, escorting them through the backstage area and down to their seats.

"Awesome," Jessica said. "Front row!"

"Anything for you, Gorgeous," Athletic Guy said.

Jessica felt someone tapping her knee. "Huh?" She opened her eyes and looked up as the daydream faded. Elizabeth was waving something in her face. "Here you go," she said. "Hot off the press."

The newspaper! Jessica grabbed it from her hands. "Thanks, Elizabeth," she said, but Elizabeth had already disappeared back into the office.

Jessica spread the newspaper out in front of her. It was still warm. She smoothed out the front page and started at the top, methodically working her way down each column.

The first page didn't have anything of interest. Neither did the second or third.

Jessica kept on, determined to read every single ad, even if it took all night. She plowed through pages four, five, six, seven, eight . . . By the time Jessica reached page sixteen, her vision was starting to blur and her hopes were starting to fade. It seemed as though Athletic Guy had given up on the whole idea of personals.

Then an ad in bold type caught her eye. Jessica let out a shriek. "Yes!" she shouted, leaping to her feet and dancing around the hallways in triumph. "Yes, yes, yes!"

It was an ad from Athletic Guy. And it was addressed to her! "Desperately seeking Gorgeous Blonde," it said. "Thanks for the awesome letter. What's your box number?"

Jessica's heart soared. Of course! When she wrote to him she hadn't told him her box number. How could she have forgotten something as important as that? He *did* like her. All this time, he just hadn't known where to find her!

Jessica reached into her backpack and pulled out her favorite purple notebook. She carefully tore out a sheet of paper. Where to start? What to say?

She decided to just plunge right in. "Dear Athletic Guy," she wrote. "I was so happy to hear from you. Sorry about the box number. It's one, as in Box #1. Write back and tell me whether my guesses about you were right. Signed, Gorgeous Blonde." She rushed back to the *Sixers* office and dropped the note into Box #23. One thing was certain—she definitely knew *his* number!

*　　*　　*

The next morning Jessica ran all the way to school. When she got there, she headed straight for the *Sixers* office to check her response box. It was still empty, but she wasn't worried. Now that she knew he was interested, she didn't have to feel anxious anymore. He probably hadn't gotten to school and found her note yet. She was sure he would respond by lunchtime at the very latest.

Jessica checked her box between each class. It was still empty after first period, second period, third period . . .

Jessica checked again right before lunch. There was a note there! Her heart soared as she unfolded it with trembling fingers. It took her a second to realize it wasn't from Athletic Guy. She stared at the signature in disbelief. "Donald Zwerdling *again*!" she exclaimed aloud, startling Julie Porter, who was working at the computer. "Doesn't that guy ever give up?" She crumpled up the note and stalked off toward the cafeteria before Julie could respond.

While her friends ate and chattered, Jessica sat silently, hardly touching her chicken sandwich.

"Don't tell me you're dieting to get ready for Rick's party, too," Mandy said after a few minutes. She gestured at Ellen and Lila. "These two haven't eaten anything but carrot sticks and diet soda for days. They're really crazed about it. I keep telling them how obsessive they're being about the whole thing. It's unhealthy."

"Give us a break, Mandy," Lila snapped. "We can't all be as naturally slender as you. Some of us have to work at it."

"That's ridiculous, Lila," Mary said with a laugh. "There's not an ounce of fat on your whole body."

Lila ran her hands over her waist and smiled with satisfaction. "I guess you're right," she admitted. "I'm just a little nervous about meeting my dream guy at the party. I want to look as absolutely stunning as I possibly can."

"Me, too," Ellen agreed, chomping noisily on a carrot stick. "Did I tell you guys that I officially agreed to go to the party with my personals pen pal?"

"Really?" Janet said, leaning over to join the conversation. "You mean Tall Blond and Handsome?"

"No, the other one," Ellen said with a giggle. "The one who calls himself Stupendous Stud."

Mandy rolled her eyes. "If you go out with a guy who calls himself that, I'd ask for a money-back guarantee," she commented.

Ellen glared at her. "For your information," she said icily, "this could be the guy of my dreams we're talking about. He sounds wonderful. He hates math, science, English, and social studies, just like me."

"Sounds like a match made in heaven," Lila commented. She smiled. "Just like me and Beach Bum. I can't wait to meet him in person. I'm sure he's gorgeous." She turned to Janet. "I can't decide whether to wear my new purple tank dress or my red silk outfit to the party. What do you think?"

As the rest of the Unicorns began a spirited debate on Lila's wardrobe dilemma, Jessica sighed and got up from the table. The more the other Unicorns talked about Rick's party, the more leftout Jessica felt, since she still didn't have a date. "I'll see you guys later," she said, picking up her tray. "I've got to get going."

Her friends waved good-bye without pausing in their discussion. Jessica sighed again, then deposited her lunch tray and rushed to the *Sixers* office. There had to be a response in her box from Athletic Guy by now. There just *had* to be.

Elizabeth was bent over the computer when Jessica burst in. "Hi, Jessica," she said, looking up.

"Has anything come in for me?" Jessica said, bolting across the room toward her response box.

"To be honest, I haven't been paying much attention," Elizabeth said. "A lot of people have been in and out."

Jessica shoved her hand inside her box. Her fingers groped around the empty space until they found a small piece of folded paper. Maybe this was the note she was waiting for!

She pulled out the note and saw that it was a cleverly folded piece of green construction paper. "Box #1" was written on the front in blue glitter marker.

She carefully opened it up. "Dear Gorgeous Blonde from Box #1, We've finally connected." *It's him!* she thought ecstatically. She felt her cheeks turning pink. She read on: "By the way, you were right about roller coasters and bubble gum, only it's the pink gum I like, not the purple. And only if it's the kind that blows the big bubbles." Jessica smiled.

"Good news?" Elizabeth said.

"The best," Jessica said. "Athletic Guy finally wrote back."

"That's wonderful," Elizabeth said with a smile.

Jessica nodded happily and kept reading. "Now let me make some guesses about you," the note continued. "Besides being gorgeous, you're lots of fun, you like to party, and you have excellent taste in music. Am I right?" Jessica nodded to herself. So far, so good. She read on. "Since you're such a good guesser, try figuring this one out: There's a song on the new Johnny Buck CD that has made me think of you all week. Which one is it?" He signed the note, "Yours, AG." At the bottom was a P.S. "This stationery is being brought to you courtesy of art class."

Jessica pressed the note to her heart and glanced across the room. "Lizzie! Do you have the new Johnny Buck CD?"

"Me?" Elizabeth said, puzzled. "You're the Johnny Buck fan in this set of twins, remember?"

"Never mind," Jessica said, rushing into the hall. She spotted Olivia Davidson. "Do you have the new Johnny Buck CD?" she asked her.

"At home I do," Olivia said. "Why?"

"Can you remember the names of any of the songs?" Jessica said urgently. "It's really important."

"Um, let me think," Olivia said. "The first one is called 'Blue You'; then there's 'Angela's Song,' 'Idol Chat,' 'Roller Coaster Romance' . . ."

"That's it!" Jessica cried. " 'Roller Coaster Romance'!" Now she remembered hearing it on the radio. She began singing the words.

> "Bringin' me down
> Bringin' me up
> Rockin' me round
> Just like a pup."

Olivia joined in.

> "She's my roller coaster baby
> My roller coaster gal
> See if you can catch her
> My roller coaster pal . . ."

A few people walking past slowed down to stare. Olivia and Jessica both started laughing, which put an end to the singing. "That's a good song," Olivia said, catching her breath. "What made you think of it?"

Jessica smiled. "I didn't think of it," she said, turning to leave. "It thought of me."

"Huh?" Olivia said.

"Never mind," Jessica said, hurrying off. "It's a private joke."

That night, Jessica wrote Athletic Guy her longest letter yet. In it, she told him her favorite color (purple), her favorite flower (a pink rose), and her favorite song ("Roller Coaster Romance," of course). "The favorite song is new," she said. "Thanks to you." She also told him a few things she didn't like, "especially square dancing."

When she was all finished, she went into Elizabeth's room and read the whole letter aloud to her. "What do you think?" she asked when she was finished.

"It sounds great, Jess," Elizabeth said. "Especially the part about your family."

Jessica looked down at her letter. "What part? I don't mention you guys at all."

"I know," Elizabeth said. "I'm teasing."

Jessica blushed. "I don't want whoever it is to figure out who I am. How many people at Sweet Valley Middle School have identical twins?"

Elizabeth laughed. "You don't have to explain. I understand." She gave Jessica a hug. "I'm just glad everything is working out for you."

"Me, too," Jessica replied. "And most of all, I'm glad you're not mad at me anymore."

"That goes double for me," Elizabeth replied with a smile.

Ten

◇

Two days later, Elizabeth was in the kitchen helping her mother set the table for dinner. "Where's
Jessica?" Mrs. Wakefield asked as she pulled a pepperoni pizza out of the oven.

"Writing a letter," Elizabeth said, opening a drawer
and counting out enough napkins for everyone.

"Another letter?" Mrs. Wakefield said. "That's
three she's written this week, isn't it?"

"Four," Elizabeth replied. "She wrote one on
Monday, one on Tuesday, one on Wednesday—last
night, I mean—and now this latest one tonight."
She carried the napkins over to the table and
started laying them out.

Mrs. Wakefield shook her head. "My daughter
the scholar."

Elizabeth laughed. "Not exactly, Mom," she

said. She should know. Jessica had kept Elizabeth filled in every step of the way. The letters had been flying between her and Athletic Guy since Monday. Jessica had even read Elizabeth some parts of Athletic Guy's letters—the parts that weren't too private, of course.

Mrs. Wakefield went out to the hallway. "Jessica," she called from the foot of the stairs. "Dinner's ready."

She came back into the kitchen. "Could you find your father and Steven and tell them that the pizza's ready, Elizabeth?"

Elizabeth went into the den, where her father and Steven were watching a basketball game on TV. "Dinner," she said. Neither one of them moved. "It's pepperoni pizza," she added. They both stood up.

When Elizabeth got back to the kitchen, she heard her mother out in the front hall again. "Jessica! Do you hear me? I'm not going to call you again."

"She probably has her Walkman on," Elizabeth told her mother. All Jessica had listened to for the last couple of days was the new Johnny Buck CD. "Want me to go up and get her?"

"Would you, please?" Mrs. Wakefield said. "Tell her to hurry down before the pizza gets cold."

Elizabeth went upstairs and found Jessica lying on her bed without the Walkman, staring dreamily at the ceiling. In her hands she clutched Athletic Guy's latest letter.

"Hi, Jess," Elizabeth said, walking in. She navigated around the piles of clothing tossed on the floor and sat down on the end of Jessica's bed. "Didn't you hear Mom calling you?"

"Who?" Jessica said, lifting her head.

"Mom," Elizabeth said, tossing aside Jessica's latest copy of *Smash* magazine. "Remember her? Attractive blond woman, she lives here with us? Anyway, she asked me to tell you that it's dinnertime."

Jessica smiled and lay back on her pillows. "I'm not hungry."

"It's pepperoni pizza," Elizabeth said.

Jessica sighed. "Not pineapple?"

Elizabeth grinned. Jessica was definitely living on another planet these days. "I see you got another letter."

Jessica beamed. "He's so perfect," she said in a reverent tone. "Listen to this." Still lying on her back, she began to read from the letter she was holding. " 'Dear Gorgeous: I think about you all the time. By this I mean at school, at practice, at home, and out with my friends. Wherever I go, I imagine your beautiful face, smiling at me. Whatever happens between us, I will always carry the thought of you in my heart. Forever yours, Athletic Guy.' "

Jessica's voice trailed off.

"Wow," Elizabeth said. "That's pretty intense."

"I told you he was romantic," Jessica said.

"Is there more?" Elizabeth asked.

Jessica shook her head. "I have to write him back," she said. "How can I top a letter like that?"

"It'll be tough," Elizabeth said.

"Will you help me?" Jessica asked. "Please? You're so much better at writing than I am."

Elizabeth thought for a moment. "I can't," she said finally.

"Why not?" Jessica demanded, beginning to pout.

"Because . . ." Elizabeth chose her words carefully. "Because it has to come from you. It's the same thing as your not telling him about your family yet. This is your relationship, not mine. It wouldn't sound the same coming from me."

Jessica studied Elizabeth's face. "You're right," she said finally. "And anyway, I've gotten this far, haven't I?"

"Yep," Elizabeth said.

From downstairs they heard Mrs. Wakefield calling them. "Jessica! Elizabeth! What's going on up there? Now both of you are missing."

"Coming, Mom," Elizabeth called back. She stood up. "Sure you don't want some pepperoni pizza?" she asked.

"I'd prefer pineapple," Jessica said, stretching her arms. "But since you asked, I guess I am a little hungry. I might be able to force down three or four slices."

Laughing, they headed downstairs together.

The following Monday morning, Jessica checked her response box as soon as she got to school, as usual. "Wow," she said, pulling out a fistful of notes. She counted them. "Six letters?" she said aloud. "He wrote me six letters over the weekend?" Smiling, she pulled six letters out of her backpack and stuck them into Box #23. "There!" she said, feeling very pleased. "I guess that shows we think alike."

Jessica's correspondence with Athletic Guy continued to blossom. For the next couple of days, her response box was bombarded with dozens of notes and messages.

Then, on Wednesday, she had a special surprise. When she checked her box that morning, she found a freshly cut pink rose. "For you," the tag said. "A favorite flower for my favorite girl."

"Ohhh," Jessica said. She held it to her nose and sniffed. This proved it—Athletic Guy was the most romantic boy she'd ever known in her whole life.

Just then Lila strolled into the office. "Where'd you get the flower?" she asked.

"My response box," Jessica answered.

Lila grinned. "It figures," she said.

Later that morning, Jessica was on her way to third period. In one hand she clutched a bag of gumdrops that she'd just coaxed Winston Egbert into selling to her. She planned to drop them off in Athletic Guy's box after lunch as a thank-you for the rose.

As Jessica pushed her way through the crowded

halls she wondered who Athletic Guy could possibly be. Her eyes scanned the crowd. Who could have guessed that the guy of her dreams was walking the halls of school at that very moment?

She caught a glimpse of Aaron. He was walking alone, probably on his way to math class. Poor guy. She almost felt sorry for him. She'd gotten over him so quickly. Since their breakup, she had barely thought of him at all. Jessica shrugged. Oh, well. Those were the breaks. She couldn't waste her time worrying about Aaron—not when she had so many much more interesting things to think about.

"Hi, Jessica."

Jessica looked up to see Caroline Pearce standing in front of her. "Oh, hi, Caroline," she said.

Caroline took a step closer. "So . . . has he asked you yet?"

Jessica knew exactly what Caroline was getting at, but she pretended not to have any idea. "Who?" she asked innocently.

Caroline raised her eyebrows. "You know. Your personals boyfriend. Has he asked you to Rick's party? It's this weekend, you know."

"Yes, I know," Jessica said, fighting to keep her voice neutral. The fact was, Athletic Guy hadn't brought up the topic of the party yet at all, let alone asked her to go with him. But the last thing Jessica wanted was to tell Caroline that. "Maybe," she answered noncommittally.

Caroline didn't seem bothered by Jessica's answer. "Well, it seems like everyone in school has found a date through the personals. A lot of new couples will be meeting face-to-face for the first time at Rick's party," Caroline informed her.

"Really?" Jessica said. "Like who?"

"Well, you probably already know about Janet and Lonely Biker, and Ellen and Stupendous Stud," Caroline said, ticking each new couple off on her fingers. "And of course, there's Lila and Beach Bum, Patrick Morris and Cute Chick, Jake Hamilton and Funny Girl, Sophia Rizzo and The Joker, Mandy Miller and Awesome Dude, Belinda Layton and Jumping Jack, Amy Sutton and Rock Jock . . . and plenty more. There are so many new couples, I'm having trouble keeping track of them all." She shrugged. "Of course, the worst part is I can't figure out which personals names go with which people. But I guess we'll all find out at the party."

"I guess so," Jessica agreed, shivering a little at the thought of meeting Athletic Guy in person. *If* he ever got around to asking her to the party, that is.

Caroline nodded, looking pleased with herself. "Rick isn't even bringing Tamara. Can you imagine? He's bringing someone called Princess Charming."

"It will seem strange to see everyone with new partners," Jessica said. Things were so topsy-turvy lately. Still, Jessica couldn't help feeling optimistic about the whole thing—at least as far as she and Athletic Guy were concerned. Even though he hadn't asked her to the party yet, she wasn't really that worried. It was obvious they were the perfect couple, and she was sure he would ask sooner or later. She couldn't wait to meet him in person.

Later that same day the *Sixers* staff held a special meeting.

"OK, guys," Elizabeth said. "Let's get started." She was sitting in the office, surrounded by Amy, Sophia, Julie, and the rest of the regular writers.

She was having some trouble getting the meeting started, however, because Amy and Sophia were too busy discussing the latest notes from their personals boyfriends.

"I can't wait to meet him at Rick's party," Sophia exclaimed to Amy. "He sounds like such a great guy."

"What's his name again?" asked Julie, who was listening curiously.

Sophia sighed and smiled. "He calls himself The Joker. Isn't that cute?"

Elizabeth rolled her eyes. Normally Sophia would be the last person in the world to think something like that was cute. Obviously, she had a serious case of personals fever!

"Well, I can't wait to find out the real identity of Rock Jock," Amy said. "I mean, it's hard to believe that such a perfect guy has been walking the halls of Sweet Valley Middle School all this time, and I didn't even know it."

"That's exactly how I feel," Sophia agreed. "I can't believe I haven't met The Joker before this. He's so obviously perfect for me. I keep trying to figure out his real identity."

"I know what you mean," Amy agreed with a giggle.

"Doesn't it drive you crazy not to know who these guys are you keep writing to?" asked Nora Mercandy curiously. She, Julie, and Elizabeth were the only members of the *Sixers* staff who hadn't placed ads.

"That's part of the fun," Sophia told her. She shrugged and smiled. "I've realized that was what was missing from my relationship—if you can call it that—with Patrick. There was nothing exciting about it. We would talk on the phone, meet at the mall . . ."

"Maybe go to a movie if you're lucky," Amy supplied, nodding in agreement. "There was no *mystery* to it. It was just boring."

"Well, I still don't think I would like it," Nora said. "Just think, you're pouring your hearts out to this guy. What if he turns out to be Bruce Patman or someone?"

Amy shuddered. "There's no chance of that," she said firmly. "Bruce is stuck-up and obnoxious. Rock Jock is sweet and funny. I can tell from his letters."

"Hey, Randy Mason could be considered sweet and funny, too," Nora pointed out. Randy was a nice but very nerdy boy who usually seemed more interested in science than in girls. "But you wouldn't necessarily want to *date* him."

"Don't be so pessimistic, Nora," Sophia said. "We can tell what these guys are like from their letters, right, Amy? And it's obvious they're not jerks *or* nerds."

Julie sighed wistfully. "Your personals pen pals do sound great," she told Amy and Sophia. "Now I kind of wish I'd placed an ad myself."

Nora shook her head. "Not me," she said. "But I do hope Rock Jock and The Joker turn out to be as nice as you think they are."

"They will," Sophia said confidently. "You'll see." She and Amy continued discussing their latest notes while some of the other staff members began eagerly describing their own personals pen pals to Nora and Julie.

"Ahem," Elizabeth cleared her throat loudly. Finally, her friends seemed to notice she was trying to get started, and they quieted down. "Are we all here?"

"Everyone except Mr. Bowman," Amy said. "He's taking a personal day, remember?" She giggled. "A *personal* day! That's pretty funny, isn't it? But it's true."

"All right, then. We can fill him in later," Elizabeth said. "According to my calculations, we made nearly two hundred dollars on the special personals edition."

They all cheered.

"Thank you, thank you," Elizabeth said, grinning. "Now comes the fun part. We get to spend it."

"How?" Sophia asked.

"However we'd like," Elizabeth replied. "That's why I called this meeting. Anyone have any good ideas?

"We could buy Mr. Bowman a new wardrobe," Amy suggested with a grin.

Everyone chuckled. Mr. Bowman was famous for his wildly mismatched outfits.

"Maybe that's why he took a personal day," Sophia said. "He could be consulting with a *personal* shopper or something."

"Don't count on it," Julie said.

"*Personally*, I think Julie's right," Nora Mercandy called out. "Mr. Bowman will never change his *personal* style."

"Wait. I know," Amy said. "We can use part of the money to pay Winston Egbert to be my *personal* science tutor. The one I found is costing my parents a fortune."

"Winston would probably work for free," Elizabeth said. She couldn't help smiling at her friends' silly jokes. Everyone seemed to be in a really good mood these days.

"You may be right," Amy said. She thought for a moment. "We could install a refrigerator in here," she said.

Sophia groaned. "Get serious, Amy."

"I *am* serious," Amy said. "We're in here nearly every afternoon. Wouldn't it be nice to have our own snack machine so we didn't have to walk all the way to the gym every time we got hungry?"

"I was hoping we could think of something having to do more directly with the paper, Amy," Elizabeth said tactfully.

"Food has to do with the paper," Amy said. "I can't think straight if I'm hungry."

Elizabeth shook her head. "Anyway, I don't think Mr. Bowman would go for it," she said. "Once people found out about it, it'd be like an airport terminal in here all the time."

Just then Ellen and Lila came in to check their response boxes. "See what I mean?" Elizabeth said. "We already have too much traffic." They all laughed.

"All right," Amy said when they had quieted down again. "You must have something in mind, Elizabeth. Let's hear it."

"Actually, there *is* something I've been thinking about," Elizabeth said. "Something we could really use."

"What?" Julie asked.

"As you know, the school will be updating its computer system soon," Elizabeth replied. "As you also probably know, I've been unhappy with our current software, and I know a lot of you guys have been, too. It can't do that much, and what it can do looks boring." Everyone nodded in agreement. "Anyway, the new computers will have color monitors and incredible capabilities. I'm hoping we can use this extra money to buy some cool new software that will give us a better look." She glanced around the room. "Comments?"

"Sounds good to me," Julie said. "There's some great new programs out there, too."

"A new computer store just opened up at the mall," Sophia reported. "It's called Comp America."

"I saw that," Amy said. "Why don't we go over after school? Is everyone free?"

They all nodded.

"Then it's settled," Elizabeth said. "We'll use the extra money to buy ourselves some new software." She smiled at her friends. "That way, even if all your blind dates don't work out, at least something good will have come from this personals craze!"

Early the next morning, Jessica slipped out the front door of the house and headed to school. As she walked, she tried to remember the last time she'd left this early, but finally she gave up and just decided to enjoy the morning. She strolled along the sidewalk, noticing how the sun poured through the palm trees, showing off the brightly colored flower beds lining the block.

Humming softly to herself, Jessica stopped and plucked a pink hibiscus flower off a bush beside the sidewalk. She stuck the flower in her hair and walked on. These past two weeks had been so wonderful, she thought. Ever since she'd begun writing to Athletic Guy, her life had been different. Better. She never would have dreamed that someone she hadn't even met in person yet could be so special to her. But somehow it felt as if she and Athletic Guy had already known each other for ages. She couldn't wait to meet him; she was positive she wouldn't be disappointed. Although she *did* find herself wondering more and more lately what he would be like. . . .

Jessica sidestepped a garden hose and made her way up the drive to school. It was so early that the doors weren't even open yet, so she sat down on a smooth redwood bench beside the entrance to wait. It was the same redwood bench, she remembered suddenly, that she and Aaron had once carved their initials in. She frowned and stood up quickly, not liking the thought of Aaron intruding when she was daydreaming about Athletic Guy.

When the school doors finally opened, Jessica headed through the halls toward the *Sixers* office. She reached the room and flipped on the light.

Right away she noticed something wrapped in pink tissue paper and a gold ribbon sticking out of her response box. Smiling, she took the package out.

It was thin and flat. A tiny, gold-trimmed card fluttered from the bow. "GB, See p. 29, AG," it said.

Jessica eagerly tore off the wrapping. Inside she found a slim paperback, its cover illustrated with hearts and flowers. "Poems for Someone Special," said the title. What could this be? she thought, her heart racing with excitement.

She turned quickly to page 29, where she found

a poem entitled "The Sailor's Wish" circled in red. Breathlessly, Jessica read the poem:

Of all the faces in the world
That I would like to see,
Yours is still the only one
That always comes to me.
For though I've traveled far and wide
And met with kings and queens,
Your golden laugh and sunny smile
Stay with me in my dreams.

At the bottom of the page was a handwritten note. "Gorgeous, It's time we met. Will you go to Rick Hunter's party with me? Love, Athletic Guy." Jessica's heart started beating. This was it! The moment she'd been waiting for!

Right away, she sat down to draft her response. Her heart was pounding about ninety miles a minute now. She took a moment to calm herself, then on a sheet of notebook paper wrote, "Dear Athletic Guy, There's nothing I'd like better than a chance to meet you. I accept your invitation. I'll leave my address in your response box tomorrow afternoon before the party. Until then, Gorgeous Blonde."

Jessica copied her letter onto the sheet of her scented pink stationery that she'd stuck in her notebook that morning just in case. Then, before she sealed the envelope, she impulsively pulled the pink hibiscus out of her hair and stuck it inside the envelope. "Sweet dreams," she said aloud, sealing the envelope shut. She dropped it into Box #23 and headed for class.

Eleven

◇

The next day flew by for Jessica. All she could think about was Rick's party that evening and how she was finally going to have a chance to meet Athletic Guy. She daydreamed through her classes and sat through lunch with a faraway look on her face.

That afternoon Jessica left her final note for him: "AG, Tonight's the night! Pick me up around 8. I'll be waiting. Until then . . . GB." She jotted her address at the bottom, dropped the note in Box #23, and headed home to get ready.

No one was home when she arrived. Jessica let herself in, grabbed a can of soda from the fridge, and headed upstairs to her room. She was glad to have the house to herself. Getting ready for Rick's party was going to take every ounce of her concentration.

First, Jessica showered and washed her hair with her favorite herbal-scented shampoo. Then she carefully blew her hair dry and curled it. When she had finished, she smiled at herself in the mirror. It had come out perfectly. She hoped that was an omen for the rest of the evening. Just then, Elizabeth walked into the bathroom dressed in her robe.

"Hi there," Jessica said. "Good timing. I'm almost finished in here."

Elizabeth grinned. "I had a feeling you'd beat me to the bathroom tonight. Your hair looks nice. Do you know what you're wearing yet?"

Jessica shrugged. "As a matter of fact, I don't. I've been so busy for the past few days thinking about meeting Athletic Guy that I haven't been paying much attention to my friends at lunch."

"Really?" Elizabeth asked with a laugh. "Well, you have pretty good fashion sense, Jess. I'm sure you can come up with a great outfit even without the Unicorns' input."

Jessica frowned. "Well, of course I can," she replied. "That wasn't what I meant. I meant that now I have no idea what any of the others are wearing. I don't want to show up in the same outfit as one of my friends." She gazed at her twin distractedly. "Maybe I should borrow something of yours, Lizzie," she said. "That way I'll know none of my friends will be wearing anything like it. I should be able to put together something halfway decent from your clothes if I'm creative about it."

Elizabeth laughed. "Well, when you put it that way, how can I refuse?" she commented wryly. "Just do me one favor. Try to keep the pile of clothes you borrow separate from all the other piles in your room, OK?"

Jessica grinned. "You've got it." She went into Elizabeth's room and threw open the closet door. As usual, Elizabeth's closet was immaculate. She had skirts and dresses in one section, blouses in another, and pants in another. All her sweaters were folded neatly on the shelf.

"Too much," Jessica said to herself as she thumbed through the sweaters. Elizabeth even had them color-sorted.

Jessica pulled out a few items that interested her, including a sleeveless blue blouse and a pair of cream-colored satin flats that she found on the floor.

Then she crossed back through the bathroom connecting Elizabeth's room with her own and tossed Elizabeth's things onto her bed. She began rummaging through her own closet, which was as chaotic as Elizabeth's was neat. Jessica tossed several skirts, a pair of black leggings, and a couple of shirts onto the bed. By digging through the largest of the piles of clothes on the floor near the dresser she managed to locate her favorite purple tunic top and a brand-new pair of pants. She added them to the pile, then sat down on the bed and stared at her choices.

After trying a few combinations, she decided nothing she had found was quite right. She shoved all the clothes onto the floor and headed back to her closet. She stood staring sightlessly at the few items that were actually hanging there as she ran through her wardrobe in her mind. Maybe she could wear her bright-purple tank dress with Elizabeth's off-white cardigan sweater.

She spent a few minutes searching for the dress, which she found balled up under her bed. She shook it out and held it up. It was hopelessly wrinkled.

Jessica sighed. *I should have gone to the mall and bought something new*, she thought to herself. Lila was sure to have a brand-new outfit for tonight. She really wished she'd paid more attention at lunch that day so she'd have some idea what everyone else was wearing. It was too late to call her friends now and find out.

By thinking hard, she finally remembered that Ellen had said something about a new outfit. Apparently Ellen's blind date, Stupendous Stud, had a thing about purple flowers, so Ellen had bought a skirt covered with purple and yellow sunflowers.

Jessica bit her lip. First impressions were always so important. She wanted to look just right for her blind date with Athletic Guy. She went back into Elizabeth's room and started flipping through the hangers in her closet again.

Meanwhile, in the bathroom, Elizabeth had finished blow-drying her hair and was thinking about what to wear. She didn't usually spend a lot of time on her appearance, but tonight Jessica had gotten her thinking. *Todd is so used to seeing me in certain kinds of outfits*, she thought. *Maybe this is my chance to wear something a little more . . . exciting. Fun. Romantic.*

As she put the finishing touches on her hair, Elizabeth thought about the clothes in her closet. Nothing seemed quite right for this evening. Maybe she should ask Jessica's advice.

She put away the hair dryer and went into her sister's bedroom, but Jessica wasn't there. Just then Elizabeth heard her twin in the next room, singing "Roller Coaster Romance" for about the billionth time. "Hey, Jess," she called. "Can you come here for a minute?"

Jessica stuck her head into the room. She was wearing Elizabeth's pink cotton tank dress. "You rang?"

"Is that what you're wearing?" Elizabeth asked.

"I don't think so," Jessica said. "Why?"

"Because if you have some time, I need some help," Elizabeth said. "I want to wear something different tonight."

"Different from what?"

"Different from what I usually wear," Elizabeth said. "More party-ish."

"Oh," Jessica said, smiling. "Now I get it. I'll be glad to help." She went to her closet and pulled out a short flared turquoise skirt. "*Voilà!*"

Elizabeth looked at it doubtfully. "Well, it's cute, but isn't it kind of short?"

"That's the point," Jessica said briskly. "Come on, let's find a top to go with it." She led the way back into Elizabeth's room and started going through her clothes again. She held up a sleeveless white blouse that tied at the midriff and examined it with a critical eye. "Nice, but not for tonight," she said after a moment, tossing it aside. "What you need is a little mystery."

Elizabeth giggled. "Maybe you're right," she agreed, feeling bold and daring at the very thought.

"Wait!" Jessica said. "I have just the thing! Stay here."

Jessica disappeared into her room and returned a second later with a black scoop-necked knit top. "Try this on," she said to Elizabeth. "It's supposed to be worn off your shoulders."

"Really?" Elizabeth said. She slipped the top over her head and allowed Jessica to adjust it. "This feels weird," she said, patting her bare shoulders.

"Now let's see it with the skirt," Jessica said, ignoring her sister's comment.

Elizabeth put on the skirt and waited as Jessica looked her up and down. "Well . . . what do you think?"

"Perfect," Jessica pronounced. "You look fantastic. Just add some tights and a pair of dangly earrings and you'll be ready to go."

Elizabeth stared at herself in the mirror and then

smiled. It wasn't an outfit she would ordinarily have chosen, but now that she saw herself in the mirror she knew what Jessica meant. She felt special. Different. Mysterious. *When Todd sees me, he'll be glad* he *didn't place a personals ad!* she thought in satisfaction.

Jessica glanced at the clock. "Oh, my gosh. Look what time it is! I still haven't decided what to wear." She rushed out of the room, waving away her twin's thank-yous.

Jessica stared into her closet. What to wear? What to wear? She had to decide on something—Athletic Guy would be arriving soon. Then she remembered the perfect dress.

It was tucked away in the back of the closet, waiting for a special occasion. Jessica couldn't believe she had almost forgotten about it. Usually she wore her new clothes as soon as she got them home, but this dress had seemed to be worth saving. She pulled it out and held it up. It was a purple flowered sleeveless dress with a flared short skirt that ended above her knees.

Jessica slipped it on. The material moved gently around her as she walked over to the mirror. On the way, she slipped on the cream-colored flats she'd found in Elizabeth's room. Then she gazed at herself, a pleased smile on her face. Perfect. She fastened on her tiny gold and pearl earrings and matching bracelet, dabbed on a little lip gloss, and was almost ready to go.

"Wow," Elizabeth said when the twins met in the hallway outside their rooms. "You look great."

"So do you," Jessica said. She smiled. "If I do say so myself!"

Elizabeth laughed. "Thanks again for the fashion advice. This is a pretty big night, you know."

"Tell me about it," Jessica said, laughing uncomfortably.

"Are you nervous about meeting your dream guy?" Elizabeth asked.

"A little," Jessica said. "What if I don't like him after all?"

"Don't worry. You will."

The doorbell rang. Jessica turned pale. "Is that him already? I'm not ready for him yet!"

"Relax," Elizabeth said. "It's probably Todd. He's always early."

From downstairs, they heard Mrs. Wakefield calling. "Elizabeth. Todd's here."

"See what I mean?" Elizabeth said. She squeezed her twin's hand. "I'll see you at the party. Good luck."

"Thanks, Lizzie," Jessica said.

Elizabeth got ready to make her entrance. She slowly walked down the stairs, feeling poised and elegant. Todd was waiting for her at the bottom. She watched him look up. His eyes grew wide. His chin dropped. "Elizabeth?"

"Hi, Todd," she said in her most mature-sounding voice.

Todd was speechless for a moment. "Wow," he finally said. "You look great. Did you do something different to yourself tonight?"

"A little something," she said mysteriously.

Todd held out his elbow and smiled, his eyes not leaving her for a second. "Shall we?"

"My pleasure," she said, taking his arm.

Upstairs, Jessica touched up her hair one last time, put on some more lip gloss and a touch of mascara, and hurried into her mother's room to borrow a tiny dab of perfume. Then she took a long, deep breath. Now she was absolutely, totally ready.

For five long minutes she anxiously paced up and down the downstairs hallway waiting for Athletic Guy to arrive. Her stomach was in knots.

Finally, the doorbell rang. "I'll get it," she called out.

Jessica walked slowly to the door, worried that her heart was going to jump right out of her chest. Could Athletic Guy possibly be as wonderful as she thought he'd be? What if he was too short? Too weird? Nothing like he described himself? What if it was some nerd just pretending to be cool?

She reached for the doorknob. On the other hand, what if he really was the guy of her dreams?

A guy even more unbelievably wonderful than she was hoping?

Jessica took one final deep breath, then opened the door. She kept her eyes lowered flirtatiously for a second, then looked up to find herself staring at . . .

Aaron Dallas!

Jessica blinked, then gasped. Aaron? *Aaron* was Athletic Guy? It couldn't be! Or could it?

She stared at him in amazement. She felt her heart start to pound all over again. Suddenly it all made sense. *Aaron was Athletic Guy!* Why hadn't she figured it out earlier? He was nervously clutching an enormous bouquet of flowers.

"For you," he said, thrusting the pink roses at her. He gave her a huge, lopsided grin. Aaron's special grin. He looked absolutely adorable.

A smile spread slowly across Jessica's face. She realized she'd completely forgotten how romantic Aaron could be. And how sweet. And how thoughtful. And how wonderful. But these last few weeks, without her even knowing who he was, he'd proved it all over again. He was a pretty special guy, and she was lucky to have him. She was maybe even the luckiest girl in the world.

Aaron was gazing at her. "You look really great tonight," he said sincerely.

"Thanks," Jessica said. "So do you." She was still in a partial state of shock. "I never knew you liked pineapple pizza." It was a stupid comment, but it was all she could think of.

Aaron smiled at her. Apparently, he didn't think it was stupid at all. "*I* never knew *you* liked pineapple pizza, either," he said softly. "I guess we had even more in common than we thought, huh?"

Jessica smiled back. Than another thought occurred to her. "Before tonight, did you know it was me?"

"I figured it out about a week ago," Aaron said. "I was glad it was you."

Jessica's heart began to pound. "I'm glad it's you, too."

Aaron leaned down and whispered in her ear. "Shall we go to Rick's party?"

"I'd love to," Jessica whispered back. Still clutching the roses, she floated out the front door with him, the happiest girl in the world.

Twelve

◇

Elizabeth and Todd were among the first people to arrive at Rick's house. "Come on in," Rick said when they got there. Elizabeth was surprised to see Sophia hovering right behind Rick.

"Sophia! What are you doing here so early?" she exclaimed.

Sophia's eyes darted around the room. "I . . . um . . . came with Rick," she stammered.

Elizabeth looked from Sophia to Rick and back again. "You did?" She couldn't hide her surprise. Rick and Sophia had completely different interests— and friends.

Sophia shrugged. "We met through the, uh, personals."

"Oh." Elizabeth glanced at Todd. He smiled at her when Rick and Sophia weren't looking, and

Elizabeth stifled a giggle. It definitely looked as though *this* particular personals pairing wasn't going to work out too well!

Rick looked uncomfortable. "The party's downstairs in the rec room," he said, heading for the stairs with Sophia trailing behind him.

"Fine," Elizabeth said. She and Todd followed as well.

The Hunters' rec room was enormous. At one end sat a big pool table, where several eighth-grade boys were already cuing up. Another area featured a TV and a VCR, along with several brown plaid couches. A long coffee table in front of one of the couches held bowls of chips and pretzels and dip. A shelf on the wall was lined with sports trophies. "There's soda in the cooler in the corner," Rick said, pointing. Upstairs, the doorbell rang. "Gotta go."

He left Sophia standing in the middle of the room with Todd and Elizabeth. "Come sit with us," Elizabeth said, taking a seat on one of the sofas.

"Thanks," Sophia said gratefully. "I don't think Rick is too thrilled to be stuck with me. He sounded so different from this in his letters."

"Forget about Rick," Todd said. "You'll have more fun with us."

And for the next few minutes Todd, Elizabeth, and Sophia *did* have lots of fun. They watched in amazement as one odd couple after another showed up. First Kimberly Haver stalked in, followed by Charlie Cashman. Charlie had a big goofy grin on his face. He kept trying to put his arm around Kimberly, and she kept shrugging him off, an annoyed look on her face.

Elizabeth giggled as she watched. "Look, Sophia. You could have done worse!"

Next Jim Sturbridge came in with Melissa McCormick. Elizabeth liked both of them, but she couldn't imagine a more mismatched couple. Melissa was quiet and sensitive and very involved in volunteer work with several local charities. Jim, on the other hand, never seemed to think about anything except sports.

"So that's who Teammate is," Sophia said. "I kept telling Melissa it sounded like a sports nickname, but she was sure it meant he liked to help other people out."

Elizabeth chuckled, but at the mention of sports her thoughts had turned to Jessica and Athletic Guy. Despite how angry Elizabeth had been at her twin for starting this whole personals craze, she now hoped with all her heart that Jessica wouldn't be disappointed by her mystery date. Right now it was looking as though the odds weren't very good, though—at least judging by some of the disastrous couples who were still coming down the stairs.

"Is that really Mary Wallace with—Jerry McAllister?" Todd asked in disbelief, staring at an entering couple.

"Believe it or not, it is," Elizabeth confirmed. Jerry McAllister was Charlie Cashman's friend, and just the opposite of friendly, poised, sensitive Mary.

"Wow," Sophia said, wide-eyed. "I think you were right, Elizabeth. I *did* get off easy with Rick."

"Uh-oh," Todd said. "I think the couple of the year just came in."

Elizabeth and Sophia tried hard not to giggle as they saw a disgruntled Belinda Layton entering the party with Winston Egbert at her side.

"Don't we look cute together?" Winston asked them. He grabbed Belinda's hand and fluttered his eyelashes.

"Oh, just stop it!" Belinda sputtered. Then her eyes fell on Jim, who was now making polite conversation with Melissa over near the cooler, and her face grew red.

"Uh-oh," Sophia said under her breath. They all knew that Belinda and Jim had been going out until the personals craze had started.

Jim glanced over and spotted Belinda, and his face turned just as red as hers. But he pretended not to notice her, and just kept talking to Melissa, who looked embarrassed to be caught in the middle.

"Come on, Winston." She stalked off toward the refreshment table with Winston at her heels.

Elizabeth didn't think things could get any stranger—that is, until Janet Howell and Ken Matthews came downstairs together along with Mandy Miller and Jake Hamilton. Not one of them was smiling.

"Whoa," Sophia said, watching the four of them. "Talk about weird combinations." Janet towered over Ken by about six inches.

"Wait until Amy sees that Ken got stuck with Janet Howell," Elizabeth said. "Poor Ken."

"That's nothing," Sophia said. "Wait until Lila finds out that Mandy is with Jake. I bet she'll have a fit." They started giggling.

The two new couples came over to the sofa area. "Hi, guys," Todd said, elbowing Elizabeth. "Have a seat."

"That's OK," Ken said. "I'm going to watch the guys playing pool." He bolted for the other side of the room.

Janet watched him go with a frown on her face, then looked around "Is your sister here yet?" she snapped at Elizabeth. "I really want to thank her for her great idea about these personal ads." Without waiting for an answer, she headed for the other side of the room and joined Belinda and Winston.

"Yikes," Elizabeth said to Mandy and Jake. "She doesn't seem too happy."

Mandy shrugged. "She'll get over it." She and Jake took a seat on the other sofa. "So," Mandy said to Jake. "How did you come up with the name Awesome Dude?"

"It fit me," Jake said.

"Oh," Mandy said. "I should have known."

At that moment, Lila walked in with Denny

Jacobson. Immediately, her eyes fastened on Jake and Mandy, and she scowled.

"Look out," Todd said to Elizabeth under his breath.

With Denny trailing behind her, Lila marched over to the sofa. "What do you think you're doing?" she said to Mandy.

Mandy turned pale. "Talking," she said.

"Good," Lila said, squeezing herself between Mandy and Jake. "I'll join you."

Denny stood there helplessly for a moment. Then he noticed Janet standing alone in the corner beside the cooler. His face brightened. "I'm going for a soda," he told Lila and hurried off.

Todd turned to Elizabeth. "Some party, huh?"

Elizabeth laughed. "I have a feeling we won't see too many personal ads after this."

"Where's Jessica?" Todd asked.

"I was wondering the same thing," Elizabeth said. "I hope everything's OK." She noticed Amy walk in with Patrick Morris. "Patrick is Rock Jock?" She glanced at Sophia, who was biting her lip. Elizabeth knew that Sophia had liked Patrick for a while.

Elizabeth waved at Amy, but Amy didn't see her. Instead, she was watching Ken, who was still over by the pool table.

Moments later, Donald Zwerdling arrived— alone. In his hand he clutched a large bouquet of purple straw flowers.

"I wonder who he's waiting for?" Elizabeth commented to Todd and Sophia.

A second later Ellen Riteman burst into the room, also carrying purple straw flowers.

"Uh-oh," Elizabeth said.

Ellen glanced breathlessly around the room until she spotted the other bouquet of purple flowers. And then she spotted Donald, grinning from ear to ear.

He waved his bouquet at Ellen. "Match mates," he cried, flashing her a toothy smile.

Ellen gasped, horrified. "You're Stupendous Stud?"

Donald lifted his eyebrows up and down. "That's right, California Babe. Let's boogie."

Ellen looked as though she were about to faint. "Get me out of here!" she shrieked. She started for the stairs but then stopped to let someone pass. Her face had a startled expression as she stepped aside.

"Oh, my gosh," said Elizabeth said with a gasp. "Look who's finally here. And look who she's with!"

Everyone in the room suddenly stopped talking as Jessica and Aaron made their entrance, arm in arm.

"I don't believe it!" Elizabeth said under her breath. "Aaron was Athletic Guy?"

The room began to buzz. Everyone was whispering about Aaron and Jessica.

"I thought they broke up," Elizabeth heard someone say.

"They did," said someone else. "She met him again through her personal ad."

"Look at those flowers," Janet said in a hushed voice. "He gave her flowers."

Jessica didn't seem to notice the talk. She and Aaron drifted to one side of the room, their eyes still locked together.

"Well! At least one person here is happy," huffed Ellen in a loud voice.

Amy came up to Elizabeth and the others. "Hi," she said glumly. "Do you guys have room for one more?"

"Sure," Elizabeth said, scooting over. Amy squeezed herself onto the end of the couch.

"What happened to Patrick?" Elizabeth asked her.

"Who knows?" Amy said. She fixed her eyes on Ken again, who was now playing pool.

"I guess your perfect match didn't turn out too well, huh?" she said sympathetically.

"You can say that again," Amy said. "I mean, I've always liked Patrick, but not as a boyfriend. No offense," she added quickly, seeing Sophia's eyes narrow. "He's really nice. He's just not for me." She gazed at Ken again and sighed.

"It's pretty funny," Elizabeth said philosophically. "The only happy new couple is an old couple." She looked around. "Hey! Where'd Jess and Aaron go, anyway?"

The others looked around, too. "I guess they must have taken off," Todd said finally.

"Too bad," Amy said with a sigh. "This party could have used a little romance."

Elizabeth felt Todd squeeze a little closer to her on the sofa. She smiled. She felt bad that her friends' dates hadn't worked out. But this party had just the right amount of romance for her.

A short time later, in a corner booth in Guido's Pizza Palace, Jessica and Aaron were sitting side by side, gazing deeply into each other's eyes. Jessica sighed. She'd never realized before what beautiful long eyelashes Aaron had.

A waiter wearing one of Guido's trademark red and white striped shirts walked up. "Excuse me," he said. "Large pizza with extra pineapple?"

"Right here," Aaron said, motioning to the table.

The waiter put the pizza down. "Anything else?"

"No," Jessica said, keeping her eyes on Aaron. "Everything's just perfect, thank you."

Two weeks later Elizabeth was sitting in the *Sixers* office admiring the paper's new format. "This is so cool," she said to Amy, who was sitting beside her. "See how the masthead stands out now? This new software really makes a difference in the way the paper looks. There's so much more we can do with it."

"I know what you mean," Amy said. "I guess we were right to take new software instead of a refrigerator." She patted her stomach. "Although my stomach might not agree."

Elizabeth smiled. This was the paper's second edition with the new format. To her surprise and pleasure, the circulation had remained as large as it had been during the personals craze. "I guess the new look was a good idea. Even though we haven't received a single personal ad since Rick's party, we're still printing just as many papers. People really seem to appreciate the improved layout."

"I've noticed," Amy said, flipping through the pages. She paused on the second page. "I've also noticed that Caroline's gossip column has been twice as long as usual for the past couple of weeks. Listen to this." She began to read aloud. " 'Well, folks, it looks as though all the old couples are back together. . . . Mandy and Peter, Sophia and Patrick, Belinda and Jim, Lila and Jake, Amy and Ken . . .' "

Amy laughed self-consciously and then continued. " 'Even Janet and Denny have been seen sharing a Casey's Colossus. A certain sixth grader has been having a hard time shaking her party date, though. Seems he's been leaving purple flowers in front of her locker every day for the past two weeks. Who knows? Maybe persistence will win the prize.' "

Elizabeth and Amy looked at each other and burst out laughing. "Poor Donald," Amy said, holding her stomach. "He just doesn't know when to quit, does he?"

A few days later, Jessica and Lila were at the mall after school, looking at shoes.

"Jake invited me to the movies this weekend," Lila said. "Maybe you and Aaron can come. I think we'll go for pizza afterward."

Jessica picked up a brown sandal from the sale table and checked out the price. *Fifty dollars! Forget it!* She turned her attention back to Lila. "What are you going to see?"

"I'm not sure," Lila said. "There's a new kung fu movie that Peter Jeffries told Jake about."

Jessica laughed. "I hope he didn't take Mandy."

"I think he saw it during the time they were broken up," Lila said. "Isn't it funny how everyone got back together again?"

"I guess the old couples were just meant to be together after all," Jessica said.

"Jake has been so sweet since we got back together," Lila said. "He calls me every single night."

"That's great," Jessica said. "Who knows, maybe breaking up for a little while was actually good for your relationship." She smiled. "I know it was definitely excellent for Aaron's and mine. He called me *three* times last night."

"Hey! That reminds me," Lila said. "Guess what Daddy just got me? Three-way calling."

"Really?" Jessica said. "You mean you can talk to two people on the phone at once?"

"That's right. So if I'm talking to you and Jake calls, then we can all talk together. Or you and me and Ellen can decide to talk at the same time. Or anyone."

Wow, thought Jessica. *If I had three-way calling, I could actually save phone time since I wouldn't have to call Lila and Ellen separately.*

"What do you have to do to get three-way calling?" Jessica asked Lila, already picturing how wonderful it would be to have it.

"It's easy. You just call the phone company and tell them you want it."

Jessica picked up another pair of shoes. "Really?" Her father was always saying she spent too much time on the phone. Maybe this was the solution. "Is it expensive?"

"I don't think so," Lila said with a shrug. "You should talk your parents into getting it."

"I think I will," Jessica said. "Tonight."

Lila fingered a pair of black suede boots. "Wouldn't it be fun if *all* the Unicorns had three-way calling?"

The more Jessica thought about it, the more she liked the idea. "Yeah," she said. "Just think of all the stuff we could talk about. Boys, clothes, boys . . ."

They both laughed.

"Tonight," Lila said. "Promise you'll ask them tonight."

"I will," Jessica said. "This is something I think they'll really go for!"

What will happen when Jessica gets three-way calling? Find out in Sweet Valley Twins and Friends #80, The Gossip War.

SIGN UP FOR THE SWEET VALLEY HIGH® FAN CLUB!

Hey, girls! Get all the gossip on Sweet Valley High's® most popular teenagers when you join our fantastic Fan Club! As a member, you'll get all of this really cool stuff:

- Membership Card with your own personal Fan Club ID number
- A Sweet Valley High® Secret Treasure Box
- Sweet Valley High® Stationery
- Official Fan Club Pencil (for secret note writing!)
- Three Bookmarks
- A "Members Only" Door Hanger
- Two Skeins of J. & P. Coats® Embroidery Floss with flower barrette instruction leaflet
- Two editions of *The Oracle* newsletter
- Plus exclusive Sweet Valley High® product offers, special savings, contests, and much more!

Be the first to find out what Jessica & Elizabeth Wakefield are up to by joining the Sweet Valley High® Fan Club for the one-year membership fee of only $6.25 each for U.S. residents, $8.25 for Canadian residents (U.S. currency). Includes shipping & handling.

Send a check or money order (do not send cash) made payable to "Sweet Valley High® Fan Club" along with this form to:

SWEET VALLEY HIGH® FAN CLUB, BOX 3919-B, SCHAUMBURG, IL 60168-3919

NAME _____
(Please print clearly)

ADDRESS _____

CITY _____ STATE _____ ZIP_____
(Required)

AGE _____ BIRTHDAY_____ /_____ /_____

Offer good while supplies last. Allow 6-8 weeks after check clearance for delivery. Addresses without ZIP codes cannot be honored. Offer good in USA & Canada only. Void where prohibited by law.
©1993 by Francine Pascal   LCI-1383-123